✔ KU-649-135

Ian Livingstone

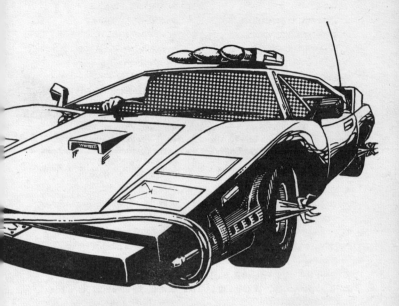

FREEWAY FIGHTER

Illustrated by Kevin Bulmer

Puffin Books

95-55

PUFFIN BOOKS

Published by the Penguin Group
Penguin Books Ltd, 27 Wrights Lane, London W8 5TZ, England
Penguin Books USA Inc., 375 Hudson Street, New York, New York 10014, USA
Penguin Books Australia Ltd, Ringwood, Victoria, Australia
Penguin Books Canada Ltd, 10 Alcorn Avenue, Toronto, Ontario, Canada M4V 3B2
Penguin Books (NZ) Ltd, 182–190 Wairau Road, Auckland 10, New Zealand

Penguin Books Ltd, Registered Offices: Harmondsworth, Middlesex, England

First published 1985
13 15 17 19 20 18 16 14

Printed in England by Clays Ltd, St Ives plc
Filmset in 11/13pt Linotron Palatino

For Ronnie

CONTENTS

Personal Abilities

As in previous Fighting Fantasy Gamebooks, your abilities will be determined by dice rolls and entered on your *Adventure Sheet* on pages 18-21. Your three abilities are as follows.

Skill

Roll one die. Add 6 to this number and enter the total in the SKILL box on the *Adventure Sheet*. Your SKILL score is a measure of your driving, mechanical and fighting abilities. SKILL may increase or decrease slightly during your journey, but may never exceed its *Initial* value.

Stamina

Roll two dice. Add 24 to the number rolled and enter the total in the STAMINA box on the *Adventure Sheet*. Your STAMINA score is a measure of your physical fitness and constitution. Your STAMINA score will reduce as injuries are sustained. The Med-Kit in your jacket contains ten packs of medical supplies to help heal wounds. Using the Med-Kit restores 4 STAMINA points. You may use the Med-Kit at any time except when engaged in combat, but remember to deduct a pack from your *Adventure Sheet* each time you use the Med-Kit. Remember also that your STAMINA score may never exceed its *Initial* value.

Luck

Roll one die. Add 6 to this number and enter the total in the LUCK box on the *Adventure Sheet*. Your

LUCK score is a measure of fate and fortune in your life. At various times during your journey, either in combat or when you come across situations in which you could either be lucky or unlucky (details of these are given on the pages themselves), you may call on your LUCK to make the outcome more favourable. But beware! Using LUCK is a risky business, and if you are unlucky, the results could be disastrous.

The procedure for using your LUCK is as follows: roll two dice. If the number rolled is equal to or less than your current LUCK score, you have been Lucky and the result will go in your favour. If the number rolled is higher than your current LUCK score, you have been Unlucky and you will be penalized.

This procedure is known as *Testing your Luck.* Each time you *Test your Luck*, you must subtract 1 point from your current LUCK score. Thus you will soon realize that the more you rely on your LUCK, the more risky this will become. Additions to your LUCK score may be awarded during your journey when you have been particularly lucky. Remember that your LUCK score may never exceed its *Initial* value.

Car Specifications

Your car's armour and weaponry will also be determined by dice rolls and entered on the *Adventure Sheet*. Its two main features are as follows:

Firepower

Roll one die. Add 6 to this number and enter the total in the FIREPOWER box on the *Adventure Sheet*. The FIREPOWER score is a measure of the car's engine power and the effectiveness of its machine-guns. FIREPOWER may increase or decrease during your journey, but may never exceed its *Initial* value. (The use of the car's rocket-launcher is explained below under 'Vehicle Combat'.)

Armour

Roll two dice. Add 24 to this number and enter the total in the ARMOUR box on the *Adventure Sheet*. The ARMOUR score is a measure of the car's defences.

In addition to its machine-guns and an unlimited supply of bullets, the car also carries missile weapons which may be used during combat. You have at your disposal four rockets (see 'Vehicle Combat'), and three canisters of iron spikes and two rear-mounted oil sprays with one canister of oil each, which may be used when the option is given. These missiles must be crossed off your *Adventure Sheet* when used.

Fuel may be acquired during the journey and should be entered on the *Adventure Sheet* in the space provided. Other modifications to and accessories for your car, which are acquired during the journey, should also be entered on the *Adventure Sheet*. ARMOUR may increase or decrease during the adventure as a result of damage or repairs to your Interceptor, but may never exceed its *Initial* value.

Combat

During your journey, you will certainly encounter some nasty characters who will attack you either while you are driving or when you are on foot. In gaming terms, there are three types of simultaneous combat.

Hand Fighting

Hand Fighting covers all non-missile hand-to-hand combat including hand-held weapons such as a baseball bat. The combat sequence for Hand Fighting is as follows:

1. Roll two dice. Add your opponent's SKILL score to the roll. The resulting total is your opponent's Attack Strength.
2. Roll two dice. Add your SKILL score to the roll. The resulting total is your Attack Strength.
3. If your opponent's Attack Strength is higher than your own, you have been hit. Proceed to step 6.
4. If your Attack Strength is higher than your opponent's, you have hit him or her. Proceed to step 6.
5. If both Attack Strengths are equal, both attacks have missed. Start the next Attack Round from step 1 above.
6. A successful hit causes injury which is represented by deductions from the injured party's STAMINA score. A bare-handed punch reduces a person's STAMINA by 1 point, but hand-held weapons such as a baseball bat cause additional injuries as ruled.

7. Start the next Attack Round (repeat steps 1–6 above) and continue until either you or your opponent has suffered the loss of 6 STAMINA points.
8. If your opponent is the first to lose 6 STAMINA points, he or she will be knocked out and you will be able to continue your journey.
9. If you are the first to lose 6 STAMINA points, you will be knocked out and will learn of your fate at the next reference you are sent to. Of course, if during Hand Fighting your STAMINA is reduced to zero, you will be dead.

Shooting

Shooting rules cover hand-guns, rifles, throwing-knives, bows and arrows, etc. (Your own revolver is assumed to have unlimited ammunition.) The combat sequence for shooting is as follows:

1. Roll two dice. Add your opponent's SKILL score to the roll. The resulting total is your opponent's Attack Strength.
2. Roll two dice. Add your SKILL score to the roll. The resulting total is your Attack Strength.
3. If your opponent's Attack Strength is higher than your own, you have been hit. Proceed to step 6.
4. If your Attack Strength is higher than your opponent's, you have hit him or her. Proceed to step 6.
5. If both Attack Strengths are equal, both attacks have missed. Start the next Attack Round from step 1 above.

6. A successful hit causes injury which is represented by deductions from the injured party's STAMINA. Missile weapons cause varying amounts of injury. Roll one die and deduct this number from the injured party's STAMINA. This is to reflect the fact that a bullet, for example, might cause only a minor flesh wound, or could kill outright.
7. Start the next Attack Round (repeat steps 1–6 above) and continue until either your own or your opponent's STAMINA score is reduced to zero (death).

Vehicle Combat

Vehicle Combat usually refers to machine-gun battles between vehicles. Your Interceptor has a turret-mounted, computer-controlled machine-gun that can fire in all directions. The sequence for Vehicle Combat is as follows:

1. Roll two dice. Add the FIREPOWER score of your opponent's vehicle to the roll. The resulting total is your opponent's Attack Strength.
2. Roll two dice. Add the FIREPOWER score of your Interceptor to the roll. The resulting total is your Attack Strength.
3. If your opponent's Attack Strength is higher than your own, your Interceptor has been hit. Proceed to step 6.
4. If your Attack Strength is higher than your opponent's, you have hit his or her vehicle. Proceed to step 6.

5. If both Attack Strengths are equal, both attacks have missed. Start the next Attack Round from step 1 above.
6. A successful hit causes damage to a vehicle which is represented by deductions from its ARMOUR score. Roll one die and deduct this number from the vehicle's ARMOUR score.
7. Start the next Attack Round (repeat steps 1–6 above) and continue until the ARMOUR score either of your Interceptor or of your opponent's vehicle is reduced to zero (destroyed). It is assumed that the driver of a destroyed car is automatically killed in the resulting crash or explosion.

If, during Vehicle Combat, you wish to launch a rocket at a target instead of firing your machine-gun at it, you may do so before the start of any Attack Round, remembering to delete one rocket from your *Adventure Sheet*. A hit will be automatic and will destroy any target.

Credits

Credits are the emergency currency units of the twenty-first century, known familiarly as 'creds'. You start your journey with 200 Credits (see your *Adventure Sheet*), but are likely to spend and/or acquire more Credits along the way. However, most people distrust Credits and prefer to barter. You may, for instance, have to use some of your Med-Kit in barter; if so, delete what you spend from your *Adventure Sheet* as usual.

ADVENTURE SHEETS

DRIVER'S NAME:

SKILL ☐
Current Skill:

STAMINA ☐
Current Stamina:

LUCK ☐
Current Luck:

EQUIPMENT LIST:

MED-KIT
(Delete as used)

+	+
+	+
+	+
+	+
+	+

CREDITS: 200

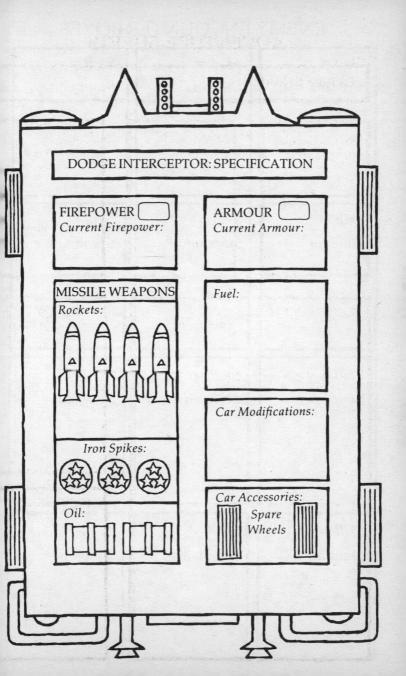

ENEMY ENCOUNTER BOXES

Skill = *Stamina* =	*Skill* = *Stamina* =	*Skill* = *Stamina* =
Skill = *Stamina* =	*Skill* = *Stamina* =	*Skill* = *Stamina* =
Skill = *Stamina* =	*Skill* = *Stamina* =	*Skill* = *Stamina* =
Skill = *Stamina* =	*Skill* = *Stamina* =	*Skill* = *Stamina* =

VEHICLE ENCOUNTER BOXES

Firepower = *Armour =*	*Firepower =* *Armour =*	*Firepower =* *Armour =*
Firepower = *Armour =*	*Firepower =* *Armour =*	*Firepower =* *Armour =*
Firepower = *Armour =*	*Firepower =* *Armour =*	*Firepower =* *Armour =*
Firepower = *Armour =*	*Firepower =* *Armour =*	*Firepower =* *Armour =*

VID NEWS BULLETIN

DATELINE 21 JULY 2022

The disaster happened just at a time when the world was beginning to enjoy itself. Nobody could have predicted such a catastrophe. World War III had been averted and the power blocs of East and West were now working towards world peace and unity. Revolutionary farming techniques had all but eradicated hunger, and increased mobility had led to people's greater understanding of one another.

The morning of 21 July 2022 had started just like any other. It was going to be a hot day and the news on the holovision was good. A government spokesman proudly announced that solar energy now powered 90 per cent of homes and 70 per cent of industry, the three-day working week was now the norm, and England was to play the United States in the soccer finals of the World Cup in Sydney. However, there were only hours to go before the beginnings of the collapse of civilization.

Later that day, an unknown disease broke out in New York, and spread with such devastating speed and fatality that before the government and scientists realized what was happening, half the population was dead. The disease spread throughout the world, carried by aeroplane passengers, and decimated population centres everywhere. All attempts at quarantine were useless. Four days after the outbreak, 85 per cent of the world's population were dead. Communications, essential services, transport and administration had broken down completely. There was no one left to try to find the cause of the outbreak. It might have been a mutated virus or some lethal germ unknowingly released from a chemical warfare laboratory. It was mere speculation and nobody really cared, as survival was the top priority.

The speed with which civilization fell into ruins was frightening. Most survivors didn't know why they still lived, and didn't know how to go on living. Brute force became the law. Riots, looting, destruction and drunkenness were commonplace. People would even kill for a can of beans. Large cities were soon abandoned due to lack of food and risk of disease.

Six months after the disaster, there remained two kinds of people – those who wanted order again, and those who revelled in the disorder. The former grouped themselves into small towns and built defences around them. Inside, they appointed leaders and began the task of self-sufficiency. These fortress towns became the homes of the military, farmers, doctors and people concerned with the rebuilding of civilization. The other group lived a wild and brutal existence outside. They were the new barbarians. Roaming the land in cycle or car gangs, they terrorized or wiped out any small pockets of civilization they came across.

You are one of the lucky survivors living in a fortress

town which has been named New Hope. You are working on the design of an early-warning system to protect the town, when you hear a knock at your door. It is two members of the town council and they look very excited. They tell you that their radio has just picked up a message from a fortified oil refinery near San Anglo in the south. The people there are willing to exchange 10,000 litres of petrol for grain and seeds to improve their food production. The inhabitants of New Hope could certainly use the petrol for generators and agricultural machinery. Being offered 10,000 litres of this rare commodity is too good an opportunity to miss, especially as there are surplus stocks of grain and seed. The council have agreed to the deal and are now looking for somebody to undertake the journey to San Anglo to deliver the sacks – and drive the petrol tanker back to New Hope. It will be a long and dangerous journey through lawless country. The two men tell you that they think you are the best-trained person to undertake such a mission, and ask if you would like to volunteer. They tell you that a Dodge Interceptor will be prepared for the journey. It will be fitted with machine-guns, radio, roof-mounted rocket-launcher, ram bars, loudspeaker and various defences, including rear oil spray, tyre-shredding spikes, armour-plating and bullet-proof windows.

You do not need convincing, as the benefit to New Hope will be enormous. This pioneer journey might be the start of the link between the new societies trying to bring about civilization – if you succeed. You tell them that you will do the job and begin your preparations immediately.

Over the next two days, you supervise the modifications to the Interceptor. When it is finally ready, it looks like a battle-car. You check it one last time to ensure that the weapons work and that all your equipment has been packed away in the various compartments. You run through the checklist: map, flashlight, Med-Kit, compass, food, water, full fuel canister, two spare wheels, Flat-U-Fix (instant puncture repairer) and tools. Finally, you put on the shoulder-holster for your revolver, and leather jacket, which carries your bullets and knife. Satisfied that you are ready, you climb into the driver's seat. Peering through the narrow steel slit that is now your windscreen, you see the town's population gathered to wave you goodbye. You start up the engine of the Interceptor and crawl forward to the gates leading to the outside world. It is over a year since you last ventured beyond the walls of New Hope, and you are excited at the prospect of what you will find.

NOW TURN OVER

1

The first thing to strike you as you cruise along the road is the speed with which everything has fallen into decay. You hadn't realized how much maintenance was needed to support civilization. All around, buildings are falling into ruin, abandoned cars litter the roads in rusted disarray, grass and weeds have grown rampant everywhere, with nobody to hold them back, and packs of dogs and other wild animals roam freely. You stop at a small town some fifteen kilometres from New Hope and switch off your engine. Suddenly it is deathly silent apart from the eerie howl of a dog somewhere down the street. You are tempted to get out of the car to explore, but realize that this is an unnecessary risk. You are about to start your engine again when suddenly the sound of a shotgun breaks the silence. If you wish to get out of the car to investigate, turn to **126**. If you would rather drive out of the town, turn to **34**.

2

You run to your car and tear open a pack of medicine from your Med-Kit. You inject yourself with snake-bite serum and dress the wound. However, the treatment does not increase your STAMINA; it merely prevents the poison from killing you. You recover some time later, but are nevertheless weakened by the ordeal. Lose 1 SKILL point and 2 STAMINA points. You walk back to the overturned Interceptor and shoot the snake with vengeful glee. Inside the glove compartment you find a few metres of coiled plastic tubing which you decide to take with you. With your arm still throbbing painfully, you drive off south again (turn to **13**).

3

You stamp down on the accelerator and release the clutch at the same time. The back wheels spin, throwing up dust, but you race off ahead of the yellow Ford. In your rearview-mirror you see the anger on your opponent's face as he drives to the limit along the narrow road to catch up with you. The Ford must be supercharged: it accelerates up behind you and rams your car at high speed. *Test your Luck*. If you are Lucky, turn to **354**. If you are Unlucky, turn to **247**.

4

You pull off the road and park the Interceptor behind a low wall. When you turn off the engine, you notice how deathly quiet it is and wonder if anybody heard you stop. You eat your food quickly but wait until it is completely dark before settling down to sleep. In the morning you wake early, feeling refreshed. Add 2 STAMINA points. You start up the Interceptor and are soon heading south (turn to **254**).

5

The front door of the motel is locked and all the windows appear to be closed. If you wish to force the lock, turn to **241**. If you would rather change your mind and spend the night inside the tanker's cabin, turn to **218**.

6

Both bikers are armed with pistols. You reply by firing your revolver, and the duel begins.

	SKILL	STAMINA
First BIKER	6	15
Second BIKER	7	17

During this Shooting Combat, both bikers will fire separately at you during each Attack Round, but you must choose which of the two you will fire at. Against the other, you throw for your Attack Strength in the normal way, but you will not wound him if your Attack Strength is greater – you must just count this as though his bullet missed you. Of course, if his Attack Strength is greater, his bullet will wound you. If you win, turn to **307**, but reduce your SKILL permanently by 1 point if you are shot more than once during the battle with the bikers.

7

Amber urges you to turn off the road and head east across the stony desert ground. She lets you drive on until the Interceptor cannot be seen from the road. Then she tells you to stop and wait until it gets dark. 'We need to be alert for our raid tonight, so I've brought along something to keep us going,' she says happily, reaching into her pocket. *Test your Luck*. If you are Lucky, turn to **319**. If you are Unlucky, turn to **136**.

8

You make as if to pass the Ford on its left-hand side, but suddenly swerve to overtake on the right. It is a successful manoeuvre and you are able to accelerate away from your opponent (turn to **340**).

9

You have made a fatal mistake by ignoring the warning. The man behind the barricade is the operator of a laser gun. As you drive forward, he presses the trigger and the narrow beam burns a hole through the steel-plated armour of the Interceptor, killing you instantly.

10

Whatever caused the tail-back certainly created havoc among the owners of the vehicles. Cars appear to have locked into other cars as frustrated drivers tried to ram their way out of the blockage, only to make it worse. You squeeze between the vehicles looking for something useful. You find a crowbar on a truck and you use it to force open the

boots of several cars. Moving up the line of cars, you suddenly panic at the thought of the Interceptor being left unguarded. If you wish to run back to your car, turn to **264**. If you would prefer to keep on searching through the cars, turn to **359**.

11

Any remaining rockets, canisters of oil and canisters of iron spikes must be crossed off your *Adventure Sheet*. The sky bandits tell you to drive off while they are feeling in a generous mood – next time they will blow up the Interceptor as well as rob you of your weapons. You curse them under your breath, but obey and drive off west. Lose 2 LUCK points and turn to **216**.

12

You know your chances are slim, but there is no alternative – this bandit has got you cold. Ignoring the pain, you roll out from underneath the ambulance and fire two wild shots at your unseen adversary. They both miss, for you suddenly see a scruffy man wearing a red headband jump up from behind a rock, returning fire at you.

HIGHWAYMAN   SKILL 8   STAMINA 12

Resolve this combat using the Shooting rules, but reduce your SKILL by 1 point for the duration of the fight because of your injury. If you win, turn to **131**, but reduce your SKILL permanently by 1 point if you are shot more than once during the battle.

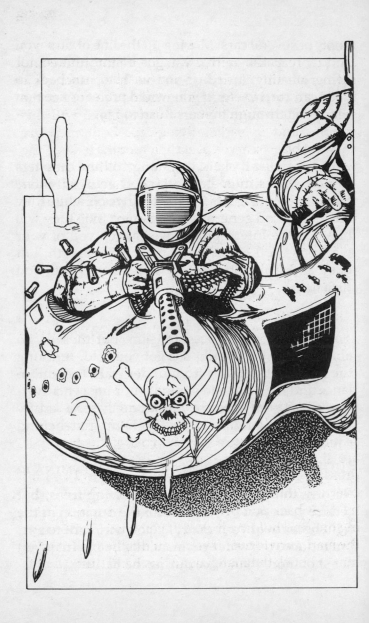

13

In your rearview-mirror you see a motor bike and sidecar steadily closing up on you. The passenger is holding a machine-gun mounted on the nose of the sidecar. He reminds you of early pilots, with his goggles and a leather flying-cap. Both men are wearing black scarves over their mouths to keep the wind-blown sand out of their lungs. When they are no more than fifty metres behind, they signal their intention by firing a burst from the machine-gun at the Interceptor. Lose 1 ARMOUR point. Will you:

Drop a canister of iron spikes (if you have one)?	Turn to **127**
Release a spray of oil (if you still have a full canister)?	Turn to **361**
Return fire with the Interceptor's machine-gun?	Turn to **282**

14

The bed is very comfortable and you do not wake up until well after sunrise. The good night's rest has left you feeling relaxed and refreshed. Add 3 STAMINA points. You run downstairs and out of the door, but are stopped in your tracks by the sight of a man dressed in white robes, emptying a petrol can all over the Interceptor. Chanting incoherent words, he steps back and produces a box of matches, striking one and holding it aloft. If you wish to call out to the man, turn to **260**. If you would rather run over to him to knock the match out of his hand, turn to **217**.

15

You walk over to the man and call out to him. He calmly turns off the torch and says, 'This is no job to be doing in the desert heat. Still, most people leave me to get on with it and don't cause me any trouble. I don't take sides, and I'll repair anybody's vehicle. If you want me to fix the damage on your car, it will cost you 200 Credits.' If you can afford the price and wish to have your car repaired, turn to **169**. If you wish to decline his offer and set off east again, turn to **259**.

16

You wake up early in the morning feeling relaxed and refreshed. Add 2 STAMINA points. If you wish to search the café, turn to **26**. If you would rather drive off immediately, turn to **254**.

17

You press your foot down hard on the accelerator to get away from the bikers before the impending explosion cripples your car. The Interceptor fishtails as the wheels spin, trying to grip the dirt. You make it past the road-block and are another hundred metres down the road before the mine goes off. It makes no more than a dull thud, but the car starts to sway all over the road, almost out of control – one of the rear wheels is virtually blown off the axle. Lose 2 ARMOUR points. You grind to a halt and jump out, revolver drawn. You see that there is no repairing this wheel and you will have to use the spare. Back down the road the bikers are starting up the armoured cycle, getting ready to attack. You climb back inside to meet them with the Interceptor's machine-guns.

MOTOR CYCLE   FIREPOWER 6   ARMOUR 9

During this Vehicle Combat, reduce your FIREPOWER by 2 because of your car's immobility. If you win, turn to **103**.

18

You shout encouragement to the citizens, but their spirit is broken. They surrender almost without resistance, and you realize that your mission will now never be completed. The Doom Dogs have their revenge.

19

It does not take long to change the wheel and you are soon driving east again. Turn to **119**.

20

Suddenly the Ford swings out to the left to try to overtake, but you have anticipated the driver's move and block him successfully. Add 1 LUCK point. You maintain your lead and, as you cross the finishing-line, the Interceptor is ahead of the Ford by half a car's length. You have won the Blitz Race (turn to **111**).

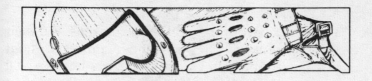

21

You do what you can to repair the car. It takes you about half an hour to clean the spark-plugs, check the oil, tune the carburettor and make sure that nothing vital is damaged. You find that three wheel-nuts are loose on one of the back tyres, and screw them up tight again. Add 2 ARMOUR points. Satisfied that everything is as well as can be expected, you set off south again (turn to **221**).

22

You flash past a road-sign which shows a turning to the south immediately ahead. If you wish to drive south, turn to **311**. If you would rather keep cruising east, turn to **203**.

23

You approach a railway bridge that you must pass under, but do not see the laughing man on top of it. A stone pillar teeters on the edge of the parapet, held from falling by the man. As he sees you drive towards the bridge, he giggles like a child and releases the pillar. It crashes down on to the road directly in front of the Interceptor. Roll two dice. If the total is the same as or less than your SKILL, turn to **137**. If the total is greater than your SKILL, turn to **342**.

24

You drive along the bumpy road until you come to a wooden gate which bars the way. The gate is covered with barbed wire and a heavily tattooed, bare-chested man sits casually astride it, brandishing a machine-gun. In a gruff voice he says, 'I don't recognize you. Which gang are you from?' 'Black Rats,' you reply on the spur of the moment. 'Never heard of them,' the man replies. 'Still, we'll race against anybody. Follow the road down to the burnt-out house and you'll see the other cars parked there. The first race will start in about five minutes. There are some pretty heavy bets being laid today. Should be lots of fun.' If you wish to drive through the gate, turn to **300**. If you would rather reverse quickly and drive back to the main road to head south, turn to **59**.

25

The force of the blast knocks you unconscious. Turn to **100**.

26

You push open the back door of the café and see that the place was looted some time ago. Broken crockery is scattered all over the floor, furniture is strewn everywhere and all the food cupboards are empty. A staircase leads up to the living-rooms, which have also been ransacked. After finding nothing of interest you walk outside but are stopped in your tracks when you see a man dressed in white robes emptying a petrol can all over the Interceptor. Chanting incoherent words, he steps back and produces a box of matches, strikes a match and holds it aloft. If you wish to call out to him, turn to **260**. If you would rather run over to him to knock the match out of his hand, turn to **217**.

27

You slam on the brakes and screech almost to a halt. The Ford swerves around you and is soon accelerating away from you. As you are not allowed to use your forward-firing weapons, you decide to ram the Ford (turn to **139**).

28

You drive on to Pete's forecourt and park the Interceptor inside the workshop. Pete quickly examines the engine and says that the acceleration of the Interceptor could be improved by the addition of a supercharger. He tells you that the cost will be 100 Credits plus some medicine. If you are able to and wish to give Pete 100 Credits and two packs from your Med-Kit, turn to **141**. If you want to, or have to, decline his offer and carry on south, turn to **88**.

29

One of the stray bullets hits you in the shoulder. Roll 1 die and deduct the number from your STAMI-NA score. You wonder how long your Med-Kit is going to last if the mission is going to continue being so dangerous. When you are finally fixed up, you limp back to your Interceptor and burn up the road, heading east (turn to **22**).

30

The crossbow bolt hits you in the shoulder, and you slide back down the ladder. Roll 1 die and deduct the total from your STAMINA. If you are still alive, you ignore the pain and run back up the ladder before the hijacker has time to reload his crossbow. Your wounds stop you from using your revolver, so you move forward to wrestle with the man. Roll 1 die and add the number to your current SKILL score, but reduce the total by 1 because of your injury. Roll the die again and add the number to the hijacker's SKILL of 7. If your total is the same as or greater than that of the hijacker, turn to **74**. If your total is lower than that of the hijacker, turn to **226**.

31

The farmhouse is an easy target to compute and you are able to press the fire button in seconds. The rocket does not miss. The explosion destroys the farmhouse, sending fragments of brick and wood flying through the air. You grab the can of Flat-U-Fix and repair the puncture. When the dust has settled, you drive cautiously ahead, one finger against the machine-gun trigger. You stop alongside the burning farmhouse, but see no signs of life. You turn off the engine and wind down the window of the Interceptor. You hear the desperate cry of a man calling for help. If you wish to get out of the car to investigate, turn to **262**. If you would rather drive south out of town, turn to **353**.

32

You pack all your equipment into two backpacks and set off towards the Doom Dogs' camp. There is a full moon and it is not too difficult to make your way across the desert. Guided by your compass, you head steadily east. After an hour, you see the glow of a fire in the distance on high ground. Amber explains in a whisper that the Doom Dogs live in tents on top of a low, flat hill where their cars are parked. When you reach the hill, you find that the slope is very gentle and you are soon at the top. You lie down and survey the movements inside the camp. A group of people are sitting around the camp-fire, drinking and laughing. Two men are walking slowly around the edge of the camp on guard duty, each armed with a rifle. You decide to crawl round the side of the hill to the barbed-wire fence, to put your plan into action. You hear one of the guards above you close by, and press yourself against the side of the hill to avoid being seen. Amber inadvertently kicks a stone which rolls down the hill a few metres. The sound it makes is very loud in the quiet of the desert night. *Test your Luck*. If you are Lucky, turn to **76**. If you are Unlucky, turn to **160**.

33

It takes a long time to dig your car out of the ditch, and it is also very tiring work. Lose 1 STAMINA point. When you are at last free, you drive off south, passing the burning wreck of the armoured car (turn to **47**).

34

You are soon out of town, zigzagging around wrecked cars and fallen trees along the road. Further ahead you can see that the road joins the main highway south. There is a small filling-station at the junction, named Joe's Garage. You stop, as you are intrigued by the hot-rod parked around the side, looking clean and in running condition. A young girl suddenly comes out of the office, wearing a T-shirt and blue jeans. She smiles and says, 'Hi, can I help you?' If you wish to talk to her, turn to **302**. If you would rather drive up on to the highway, turn to **167**.

35

It is a battle of nerves between yourself and the driver of the Ford. The two cars race abreast towards the bridge. Roll one die and add the number to your SKILL, making a note of the total. Roll the die again and add the number to the Ford driver's SKILL of 8. If your total is the same as or greater than that of your opponent, turn to **379**. If your total is less than that of the Ford driver, turn to **51**.

36

The dagger thuds painfully into your side. Roll one die and deduct the number from your STAMINA. If you are still alive, turn to **368**.

37

A huge boulder crashes down on top of the Interceptor's roof. Roll two dice and deduct the total

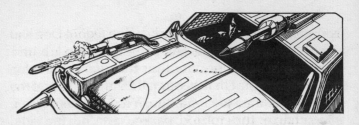

from your ARMOUR. If you survive the impact, turn
to **261**.

38

You open one of the packs inside the Med-Kit and
soon your wound is treated – pellets removed and a
layer of synthi-skin applied, with bandages to cover
it. You stand up and are about to hop back to your
Interceptor, when a huge wild dog appears at the
end of the street. Its fur is tattered from many fights
and saliva drips from its open mouth. The chances
are that it is rabid. It stoops down and then starts to
run towards you, growling as it gathers speed. If
you wish to try to shoot it, turn to **176**. If you wish to
fight it with your knife, turn to **374**.

39

Despite your injury, your reflexes are still fast. In
one quick manoeuvre, you pull the knife from its
sheath and throw it at the sneering man. A surprised expression spreads across his face as he
drops to his knees, clutching the knife handle which
protrudes from his stomach. He falls forwards,
shooting wildly as he dies. *Test your Luck*. If you are
Lucky, turn to **171**. If you are Unlucky, turn to **29**.

40

By the time you reach the tanker, the Doom Dog has already started up the engine. You jump up and grab hold of the door-handle as the man reaches for his gun. The man has a SKILL of 6 and if your own SKILL is the same or greater, turn to **81**. If your SKILL is less than 6, turn to **296**.

41

The driver of the armoured car is alert and swerves the car off the road to avoid the spikes. It powers its way through the overgrown grass verge and bounces back on to the road to continue the chase. If you wish to release an oil spray, turn to **165**. If you would rather risk a handbrake-turn to face the armoured car, turn to **77**.

42

As darkness envelops the countryside, you switch on your headlights. You drive steadily on, avoiding obstacles and occasionally picking up the gleaming red eyes of some wild animal frozen in the light. The night draws on and you begin to feel very tired. Roll two dice. If the total is the same as or less than your SKILL, turn to **161**. If the total is greater than your SKILL, turn to **186**.

43

You breathe in deeply as the Interceptor passes over the grenade. *Test your Luck*. If you are Lucky, turn to **175**. If you are Unlucky, turn to **201**.

44

'Liar! I didn't think you looked like a member of a gang. Let's hear what the others have to say.' He waves his machine-gun in the direction of the trees where his friends are sitting. If you possess a pair of knuckle-dusters, turn to **273**. If you do not have them, turn to **214**.

45

Speeding along the open road, you do not notice the iron spikes that have been laid down by highway bandits. You drive straight over them, and only realize that you have done so when a puncture makes the steering-wheel start to judder. *Test your Luck*. If you are Lucky, turn to **304**. If you are Unlucky, turn to **60**.

46

The kilometres roll by and the petrol gauge drops relentlessly down until it registers empty again. If you are carrying a full can of petrol inside the Interceptor, turn to **310**. If you have not acquired one recently, turn to **364**.

47

As the morning wears on, it becomes very hot and you notice a change in the vegetation the further south you travel. The overgrown fields turn into scrubland, and it won't be long before you are driving across the desert. A few miles further down the road, you arrive at a major junction. If you wish to turn right to head west, turn to **117**. If you would rather keep driving south, turn to **23**.

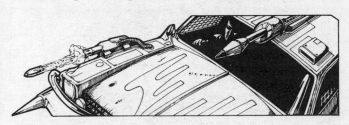

48

Gripping your knife tightly, you crouch down, waiting for the thug to make his move. Suddenly he screams and leaps at you.

THUG   SKILL 7   STAMINA 10

Use the Hand Fighting rules to resolve this combat. Both your knife and the thug's crowbar reduce STAMINA by 2 points. If you win, turn to **138**. If you fall unconscious, turn to **100**.

49

Parked in the middle of the road ahead of you is a bizarre-looking vehicle. It looks like a pick-up truck which has been converted to resemble a Roman chariot. It even has scythes attached to its wheels. A huge, bare-chested man wearing a gladiatorial helmet, which covers his face, is standing at the back of the truck holding on to a double-barrelled machine-gun. He signals to his driver to drive forward into battle. You have no choice but to fight this new-age gladiator.

CHARIOT   FIREPOWER 9   ARMOUR 15

If you win this Vehicle Combat, turn to **91**.

50

You dive at the robed man and pull him to the ground, but are unable to stop him throwing the match. The Interceptor is immediately engulfed in flames. Your anger is futile; the fanatic has put an end to your mission.

51

You are only a few metres away from the bridge when your nerves crack. You brake hard and watch the Ford race over the bridge ahead of you. Pressing down on the accelerator, you try to catch up. You see the finishing-line ahead, no more than two hundred metres away, and realize that the race is lost. The Ford crosses the finishing-line a car's length ahead of the Interceptor. Lose 1 LUCK point and turn to **232**.

52

Your rapid-firing machine-gun does not miss its target and the bike skids off the road, crashing into a tree. But the rider does not die in vain – his crossbow bolt pierces your front tyre and sends the tanker into a frightening skid. Wrestling with the steering-wheel, you just manage to keep control and slide to a halt. Trapped inside your cabin, you wait to see what the other biker will do next. He parks behind the tanker and shouts at you to leave the cabin. You reply in a few words, but leave him in no doubt as to what you think of his suggestion. 'How about a duel then? Winner takes all,' shouts the man. If you wish to agree to his proposal, turn to 164. If you would rather sit it out, turn to 190.

53

You press down on the accelerator, steering the Interceptor towards your attackers. But before you can reach them, they jump on to motor bikes and race off. If you wish to chase after them, turn to 78. If you would rather reverse, drive back to the road and turn right to head east, turn to 45.

54

You do not stop to celebrate your victory in case Leonardi is a bad loser. He does not try to follow you and gradually fades from view behind you. You pass an articulated truck which looks as if it has only recently been parked. If you wish to stop and examine the truck, turn to 104. If you would rather drive on without stopping, turn to 118.

55

You push open the back door of the café and realize that the place was looted some time ago. Broken crockery is scattered all over the floor, furniture is strewn everywhere and all the food cupboards are empty. A staircase leads up to the living-rooms, which have also been ransacked. Finding nothing of interest, you sit down to eat some of your own rations as the light rapidly fades. When it is completely dark, you lie down to sleep on the bed, with your revolver under the pillow. Roll one die. If you roll 1, 2 or 3, turn to **110**. If you roll 4, 5 or 6, turn to **14**.

56

You slip the knuckle-dusters over your fingers and spring up as quietly as possible. The expression of surprise on the guard's face is barely visible in the half-light, as he takes the full force of your blow. The force of it knocks him out instantly. You catch him as he falls, hoping that his friends do not notice what is happening. You tie him up with his own belt and leave him on the hillside. It won't be long before he is missed, so you scramble quickly up the hill to the fence (turn to **198**).

57

With incredible speed, you draw your revolver and have it pointed at the face of the man before he can even move. You tell him to drop his shotgun. You explain that you are not the person who killed his wife and son, and had only lied about being a road warrior to keep the whereabouts of New Hope a secret in case the man might lead a raid on it. The man looks suddenly excited and says, 'New Hope, you say? That's where I'm headed. Been cycling in that direction ever since the ambush. Only stopped here to get some cans of food from a supermarket back there, when some crazy dogs attacked me. Shot one of them and the others ran off. My name's Johnson, and I'm sorry about threatening you like I did, but you can't trust anybody these days.' You smile and shake hands, and he tells you that he is a builder by trade. He asks how much further it is to New Hope and whether he is likely to be let in. You reply that it is only another fifteen kilometres and his chances are good – they need skilled people. You also tell him about your mission and he warns you not to stop at Joe's Garage, which is about eight kilometres out of town. 'They ain't got no petrol. They just rob people who stop there.' You thank Johnson for the advice, wish him luck and walk back to the Interceptor. Its powerful engine roars into life when you turn the ignition key, and you screech off once again (turn to 34).

58

You climb the steps into the caravan and, after a rapid search through the cupboards, you discover a can of corned beef and a grenade. You put the grenade in your pocket and decide to eat the corned beef there and then, as you are feeling very hungry. Add 2 STAMINA points. Realizing that you are not likely to see your attacker again, you return to the Interceptor to head south (turn to **150**).

59

As you drive away, you hear the man on the gate yell, 'Chicken!' In your rearview-mirror you watch him reach into a leather bag hanging on the gate and extract a hand-grenade. He pulls out the detonator pin and hurls the grenade at the Interceptor. *Test your Luck.* If you are Lucky, turn to **73**. If you are Unlucky, turn to **121**.

60

Both of the rear tyres are punctured and you swerve to a halt. A man suddenly appears from the ditch by the side of the road, holding a bottle with a flame-lit rag at the mouth. You realize with horror that it is a petrol bomb, but there is nothing you can do to stop him throwing it at your immobilized car. Roll two dice and deduct the total from the Interceptor's ARMOUR. If you survive the explosion, turn to 135.

61

The road heads directly east and you are able to travel along it without incident until you reach another T-junction. Here you decide to turn right in order to drive south towards San Anglo (turn to 272).

62

You manage to control the speeding Interceptor and swerve round the overturned truck. Turn to 151.

63

The canister bursts open and spreads iron spikes all over the road. But the Ford is equipped with a powerful underbody air-jet which blows all but one of the iron spikes off the road. The only damage done is a slow puncture to one of its heavy-duty tyres, which slows it down just enough for you to accelerate out of range of its grenade-launcher for the moment. Up ahead you see the white house where you must turn around. You jam on the brakes and turn the steering-wheel sharply to the left. You reverse back a few metres in a cloud of churned-up dust, and then slam the gear stick forward into first to race back to the finishing-line. The Ford makes an equally swift U-turn and is soon just behind you. It powers alongside you, and the driver pulls down on his steering-wheel in order to sideswipe the Interceptor. He looks set to determine the outcome of this duel by ramming.

YELLOW FORD   FIREPOWER 8   ARMOUR 16

A successful ram will reduce a car's ARMOUR by 2 points. If you survive four Attack Rounds, turn to **334**.

64

You rummage through the bandit's clothing, but find nothing of use. You look at the Interceptor's tyres to see if they can be repaired. *Test your Luck*. If you are Lucky, turn to **242**. If you are Unlucky, turn to **313**.

65

You feel a stab of pain in your arm as one of the bullets clips you. Fortunately it is only a flesh wound. Lose 2 STAMINA points. The Interceptor starts first time and you screech away down the rough road to the main road, where you turn right at speed to head south (turn to **207**).

66

The road heads directly west and you are able to travel along it quickly, as it is relatively free of obstacles. However, your easy drive is shortlived. The road comes to a river, which it used to cross, but the drawbridge, which spans the river, is partly open, stopping you from driving across it. You judge that if you drive over it at about 180 kilometres per hour, the momentum should carry the Interceptor across the gap to the far side – but then again, it might not. If you wish to try to drive across the bridge, turn to **270**. If you would rather turn around and drive east, turn to **159**.

67

Like two jousting knights on horseback, the two vehicles sweep by each other with machine-guns blazing. After each pass, you turn sharply and charge at each other again. But suddenly the station-wagon swerves to ram the Interceptor. You turn the steering-wheel to take the Interceptor out of the path of the station-wagon. Roll two dice. If the total is the same as or less than your SKILL, turn to **200**. If the total is greater than your SKILL, turn to **248**.

68

Thanks to your supreme efforts, you manage to avoid all the obstacles on the road. As the first rays of the morning sun begin to creep over the horizon, your weariness departs and you drive on with renewed vigour towards San Anglo (turn to **254**).

69

The Doom Dogs are defeated and you are able to rest for the moment. By the time you manage to free the Interceptor from the station-wagon, the sun is rising above the eastern horizon, bathing you in warm, red light. You suddenly feel optimistic about completing your mission, and drive off south without any further delay (turn to **90**).

70

The wheels slam down on the far side of the bridge and you have to struggle with the steering-wheel to keep the Interceptor going in a straight line. You are across the bridge but travelling at high speed towards an overturned truck. Roll two dice. If the total is the same as or less than your SKILL score, turn to **62**. If the total is greater than your SKILL score, turn to **133**.

71

You press down hard on the accelerator, as the rocks and boulders crash down on to the road. *Test your Luck.* If you are Lucky, turn to **172**. If you are Unlucky, turn to **37**.

72

Opening the door trips a wire which is pulled taut around the trigger of a crossbow in the far wall. The bolt is unleashed from the bow and thuds into your shoulder. Roll one die and deduct the number from your STAMINA. If you are still alive, turn to **233**.

73

You press down on the accelerator and just manage to escape the blast of the exploding grenade. If you still wish to drive back to the main road to head south, turn to **207**. If you would rather take up the challenge of the Blitz Race after all, turn to **330**.

74

Your attacker is well trained in the art of wrestling, but you manage to flip him on to his back. You push him off the top of the trailer and watch him land heavily on the road below. He is knocked unconscious; you seize the opportunity to drive away. All day you drive as fast as the tanker will go. Apart from a disorganized ambush attempt in the late afternoon, which you easily smash through with the armoured tanker, there are no incidents on the road. It is nearly dusk when you reach the outskirts of New Hope, its high, defended walls a strange but welcoming sight. If you were bitten by a rat on your homeward journey, turn to **275**. If you escaped being bitten, turn to **380**.

75

As soon as you release the clutch you hear a loud bang – a tyre has blown. You curse and get out of the car. The girl had placed a small mine under your front wheel while you were fighting. The wheel is a wreck and you will have to put on a spare. Lose 1 LUCK point. You resolve not to be so keen to speak to strangers in future, and drive up on to the highway (turn to **167**).

76

The guard does not pay any attention to the noise of the rolling stone, being distracted by the jokes that

his friends are telling around the fire. He walks on by and you are able to crawl up to the fence (turn to 198).

77
You turn the steering-wheel sharply to the left, at the same time pulling hard on the handbrake. The tail end of the car swerves right around, and you stamp down on the accelerator to halt the skid. Roll two dice. If the total is the same as or less than your LUCK, turn to 290. If the total is greater than your LUCK, turn to 352.

78
The bikes are suited to driving along the dirt track and you are unable to catch up with them. In the distance you see a cluster of houses which must be Rockville. The bikes drive straight towards the houses and disappear from view. As you get closer you hear the sound of gunfire, which seems to be coming from the nearest farmhouse. Will you:

Fire a rocket at the farmhouse?	Turn to 199
Keep on driving towards the houses?	Turn to 377
Reverse, drive back to the road and turn right to head east?	Turn to 45

79
Your engine is still running and sounds undamaged. If you wish to stop and deal with your attacker, turn to 281. If you would rather keep driving south, turn to 150.

80

Suddenly the Ford swings out to the right to over-take; you have anticipated incorrectly and turn to the left. The Ford accelerates past and, when you cross the finishing-line, the Ford is ahead of the Interceptor by half a car's length. Lose 1 LUCK point and turn to **232**.

81

Your reactions are faster than those of the desert raider. You fling the door open and pull him out of the driver's seat on to the ground. He is easily overcome, and then you order him to tell his friends to call off the attack. He reluctantly agrees to your demand and the shooting stops almost immediate-ly. You keep your gun trained on your hostage while you watch the rest of the Doom Dogs retreat back into the desert. You let the captured Doom Dog follow his friends to the jeers and cheers of the inhabitants of the San Anglo refinery. After helping with the repairs to the entrance, you tell them that it is time for you to leave. You climb into the cabin of the tanker and wave farewell. You feel sad to be abandoning your faithful Interceptor, but realize the importance of this mission. Two cars escort you north along the road, until you reach the edge of the desert. They turn and drive back to San Anglo, leaving you alone on the highway once more. You decide to head directly north, ignoring all turnings that you come to. The day passes without incident and you keep on driving well into the night. When you are too tired to drive any further, you pull into a motel car-park, as there are no lights showing in the rooms. If you wish to sleep inside the cabin of the tanker, turn to **218**. If you wish to go inside the motel, turn to **335**.

82

Roll two dice. If the total is the same as or less than your LUCK score, turn to **39**. If the total is higher than your LUCK score, turn to **244**.

83

You dive inside the Interceptor and fire at the sky bandits overhead, who return fire immediately.

HELICOPTER   FIREPOWER 8   ARMOUR 11

During this Vehicle Combat, reduce your FIRE-POWER by 2 because of your car's immobility. If you win, turn to **305**.

84

Unknown to you, the dark and warm environment of the outhouse is the perfect habitat for redback spiders. Your disturbed dreams make you toss and turn, and your arm brushes against one of these spiders. It instinctively bites you, emptying virulent poison into your veins. Roll one die and deduct the number from your STAMINA. If you are still alive, turn to **258**.

85

You quickly snip through the wire and crawl into the compound. Amber moves from vehicle to vehicle, attaching small limpet mines to their engine blocks. When she has finished activating them, she signals for you to leave. You crawl down the side of the hill and stand up to run when you feel you are out of sight. The explosions suddenly start, and you count seven in all. 'One of the mines must have had a faulty fuse,' Amber says in a breathless voice as you run back towards the Interceptor. You hear an engine start and look behind you to see two beams of light moving away from the rising flames of the burning wrecks. The Doom Dogs intend to hunt down their attackers. If your current STAMINA is 10 or greater, turn to **107**. If your current STAMINA is less than 10, turn to **326**.

86

Your revolver is only halfway out of its holster when the stranger squeezes the trigger of his shotgun. You see a puff of smoke at the same time as your right thigh is gripped with pain. You are knocked back against the wall, the sound of the blast ringing in your ears as you slide down to the ground. Roll one die, add 2 to the number rolled and deduct the total from your STAMINA. The man turns and walks away, leaving you for the dogs. If you wish to fix your wound immediately, using your Med-Kit, turn to **38**. If you wish to crawl to the safety of your car, turn to **256**.

87

The man reacts quickly and dodges your swinging fist. Suddenly you are staring down the barrel of his machine-gun: you decide against trying to punch him again! He tells you to turn round and then brings the butt of his gun down hard on the back of your head. You crumple to the ground, unconscious (turn to **100**).

88

It is not long before the green vegetation gives way to more barren terrain, with tufts of dry grass dotted on top of the stony, brown earth. You soon arrive at the edge of the desert, where the road is joined by another main road leading east. If you wish to turn left, turn to **177**. If you would rather keep going south, turn to **271**.

89

You decide that this town is too dangerous to stay in any longer, and hobble back to your Interceptor. Back behind the wheel, your spirit returns as you release the clutch and screech out of town (turn to **34**).

Amber becomes increasingly excited as you cross the desert and see the welcome sight of the San Anglo refinery burning in the distance. When you get close, she opens the door and waves to the guards on the wall. The steel entrance doors are opened and you are allowed to drive inside. You are greeted enthusiastically by the citizens and spend the rest of the day telling them about your adventures in the barbaric outlands. You are treated as a hero, your wounds are tended and you are given the most comfortable cabin they have to offer. That night you sleep well. Add 1 SKILL point and 4 STAMINA points. In the morning you wake to the sound of gunfire. You run outside and are told that the remnants of the Doom Dogs gang are making a final assault on the refinery. You climb the steps of the wall to see what is happening outside. A small truck is being driven straight towards the steel doors, and you see the driver jump clear just before impact. There is a loud explosion and one of the doors is blown off its hinges. On motor bikes and in cars, the Doom Dogs drive straight for the breach. As the gang bursts through the wall, the citizens start to panic, and you realize you will have to take command. Roll two dice. If the total is the same as or less than your SKILL, turn to **147**. If the total is greater than your SKILL, turn to **18**.

91

You press on south as quickly as possible and switch on the radio, hoping to establish contact with San Anglo. However, no voices are audible above the crackling static. You decide to leave it on anyway, in case somebody tries to make contact with you. After driving a further fifteen kilometres, you come to another junction in the road. Somebody has left a sign there which reads 'Engine and body repairs' in crude writing, and shows an arrow pointing east. If you wish to turn left to head east, turn to **230**. If you would rather keep going south, turn to **301**.

92

You drive a long way east, passing only one junction on your left – a dirt track leading north. At last you come to a T-junction where you turn right in order to drive south towards San Anglo (turn to **272**).

93

You try to restart your stalled engine and get away before the outlaws arrive to see what they have captured. *Test your Luck*. If you are Lucky, turn to **268**. If you are Unlucky, turn to **178**.

94

You just manage to swerve round the E-type; then you press your foot down hard on the accelerator. In your mirror you see that three cars are chasing you. If you have a canister of iron spikes left, or one of oil, turn to 328. If you do not have any spikes or oil left, turn to 284.

95

Before you have time to catch them, they turn around and drive straight towards you. The machine-gun above the headlamp blazes red and white as it spits out bullets at you. You press the accelerator down hard on the floor and race the Interceptor towards them, your finger clutching the machine-gun trigger.

MOTOR CYCLE   FIREPOWER 6   ARMOUR 9

If you win, turn to 249.

96

The kilometres roll by and the petrol gauge is reading almost empty again. If you are carrying a full can of petrol inside the Interceptor, turn to 180. If you have not acquired one recently, turn to 364.

97

You stand up and walk over to where the two bikers are lying crumpled in the ditch. One of them is carrying a throwing-knife which you slide down the leg of your leather boot. You rest for a while until you feel fit enough to continue your journey (turn to 215).

98

Much to your frustration, the canister does not open and the Ford drives over it without incident. The driver retaliates by firing a grenade over your car which lands on the road in front of you. There is a muffled explosion as the steel-plated underchassis takes the full blast of the grenade. Roll two dice and deduct the total from your car's ARMOUR. If you survive the explosion, turn to 294.

99

You stop the car and empty the fuel canister into the petrol tank. You see that the Interceptor is looking somewhat the worse for wear, and wonder if it will last the trip. If you wish to carry out some instant repairs, turn to 21. If you would rather drive off immediately, turn to 221.

100

You wake some time later, your head aching worse than anything you have ever known. Then you remember – the Interceptor! You sit up and look around, but it's gone. You have failed in your mission.

101

Miraculously, you drive through the minefield without triggering off any of the mines. Add 1 LUCK point. Quite unaware of your lucky escape, you continue your journey south (turn to **303**).

102

You signal to Amber to open her door and begin firing at the Doom Dogs. Your own door is sprayed with bullets as you open it just when your four opponents begin their barrage of fire. Behind the cover of the vehicles, everybody is well protected. You aim your fire at two of the Doom Dogs, while Amber shoots at the other two.

	SKILL	STAMINA
First DOOM DOG	7	13
Second DOOM DOG	8	14

During this Shooting Combat, both Doom Dogs will fire separately at you during each Attack Round, but you must choose which of the two you will fire at. Against the other, you throw for your Attack Strength in the normal way, but will not wound him if your Attack Strength is greater – you must just count this as though you dodged his bullet. Of course, if his Attack Strength is greater, his bullet will wound you. If you win, turn to **154**, but reduce your SKILL by 1 point if you are shot more than once during the shoot-out.

103

You walk over to the wrecked bike, carrying your revolver in one hand and the Med-Kit in the other. One of the men is dead and the other is barely alive. You kick his pistol away from him and see if he can be saved. He opens his eyes, smiles and says, 'Fat Jack and the boys will get you for this.' Then he

slumps back and is still. Your Med-Kit cannot help him. You check the bike over and notice a locked side-pannier. If you wish to open the pannier, turn to **206**. If you would rather change the wheel on the Interceptor without wasting any more time, turn to **346**.

104

There is nothing of use inside the cabin, and its wagon is empty. You automatically tap the petrol tank to see if there is any fuel left in it, and are surprised to discover that there is. The tank is made of reinforced steel and you wonder how you can extract the petrol. If you have a length of plastic tubing, turn to **306**. If you do not have any plastic tubing, turn to **187**.

105

A bullet punctures your front tyre and the car grinds to a halt, directly in the path of the exploding shell. Roll two dice and deduct the total from your car's ARMOUR. If you survive the explosion, turn to **292**.

106

You circle the burning wreck and then turn south and accelerate away (turn to **47**).

107

You run like the wind, glancing several times over your shoulder to watch the vehicle circling the hill, trying to pick up your tracks. You are less than two hundred metres from the Interceptor when your tracks are spotted and the vehicle turns to give chase. An angry voice booms out over the desert through a loudspeaker, shouting, 'Stop! There is no escape from the Animal.' The message is repeated over and over again as the vehicle closes up on you. The welcome sight of the Interceptor appears before you, and you both jump inside just as your pursuers come into view (turn to **158**).

108

Much to your relief, the shot is accurate and the dog is killed instantly. Turn to **89**.

109

Whoever was driving the car must have taken everything with them when they set off on foot after running out of petrol. You walk round to the back of the car and try to open the boot, but find that it is locked. If you have a crowbar and wish to prise the boot open, turn to **277**. If you would rather give up on the police car and continue your journey south, turn to **49**.

110

You wake up early in the morning feeling relaxed and refreshed. Add 2 STAMINA points. You run downstairs and climb inside the Interceptor to drive off south without any further delay (turn to **254**).

111

The small crowd of spectators gathers around the Interceptor to congratulate you. The Ford driver climbs out of his car, slams the door shut and stomps away. 'Looks like he's a bad loser,' says one of the others, 'and it's the first time I've ever seen him lose!' The girl who started the race hands you your prize of the can of petrol which you pack inside the Interceptor. 'It'll be about half an hour before the next race starts, so we're going to sit down over by the trees. Will you join us?' she says. You decline her offer, as you are keen to carry on with your mission. They walk away, leaving you to check over the Interceptor for any serious damage. While you are bending over the engine, you feel a tap on the shoulder. You look up and see the tattooed man who was sitting on the wooden gate. 'Which gang did you say you belong to?' he asks in a hostile tone. Will you reply:

Black Cats?	Turn to **44**
Black Rats?	Turn to **156**
Black Bats?	Turn to **228**

112
Inside the general store you find a can of meat, which you greedily devour, not having eaten such a rare delicacy for a long time. Add 2 STAMINA points. More important, you find a full canister of petrol, which you stow inside the Interceptor. If you have not done so already, you may search the nearest house (turn to **252**). If you would rather drive off south, turn to **353**.

113
You fire rapidly at the advancing vehicle, and manage to shoot out both of its headlights. In the safety of darkness, you tell Amber to make a run for the Interceptor. You hear the occupants of the vehicle cursing each other as they scramble to find spare headlight bulbs. By the time they do, you are within sight of the Interceptor, and the two of you jump inside just as your pursuers come into view (turn to **158**).

114
You continue to make good headway along the country roads. The untended fields on both sides of the road have grown wild, and you wonder if they will ever be ploughed again. Still wrapped up in your thoughts, you pass by a turning on your left, but ignore it as you do not want to go north. Turn to **92**.

115

You drive for an hour, neither seeing nor hearing signs of life, until you notice two trails of dust rising into the air, one on each side of the road. They draw closer until you can see what is making the trails – two dune buggies. Both are armed with machine-guns and open fire on you as soon as they are in range.

	FIREPOWER	ARMOUR
First DUNE BUGGY	7	10
Second DUNE BUGGY	8	11

During this Vehicle Combat, both buggies will fire separately at you in each Attack Round, but you must choose which of the two you will fire at. Against the other you will throw for your Attack Strength in the normal way, but you will not damage it if your Attack Strength is greater – you must just count this as though its bullets missed. Of course, if its Attack Strength is greater, the bullet will cause damage to the Interceptor. If you win, turn to **194**.

116

The bullet hits you in the shoulder. Roll 1 die and deduct the number from your STAMINA score. In pain, you sit up and return fire.

HIGHWAYMAN   SKILL 8   STAMINA 12

Resolve this combat using the Shooting rules, but reduce your SKILL by 2 points for the duration of the fight because of your injuries. If you win, turn to

131, but reduce your SKILL permanently by 1 point if you are shot more than once.

117

You travel about eighty kilometres, and then the road ends at a T-junction. You decide to turn left in the direction of San Anglo (turn to **189**).

118

The miles slip by and your petrol gauge once again reads almost empty. If you have filled your petrol canister recently, turn to **99**. If you do not have any fuel left, turn to **364**.

119

After travelling east for another half hour, you come to a crossroads which has a main road heading south. You turn right and press your foot down on the accelerator, hoping to make good progress down the open road (turn to **272**).

120

Your shot misses, as the wolves close in to attack. You draw your knife just in time to defend yourself.

	SKILL	STAMINA
First WOLF	8	7
Second WOLF	8	8

Use the Hand Fighting rules to fight the wolves one at a time. Your knife and a wolf's bite both reduce STAMINA by 2 points. If you win, turn to **286**.

121

The grenade rolls under the Interceptor and explodes. Roll two dice and deduct the total from the Interceptor's ARMOUR. If you survive the explosion, turn to **134**.

122

Neither of the bikers saw you jump out of the Interceptor. You are able to walk around and surprise them from behind. It amuses you to watch them yelling over to where they think you are. The time is ripe to tell them where you really are. You fire a warning shot in the air and tell them to drop all their weapons. They obey immediately, deflated because you have outwitted them. You walk over to their motor cycle and notice a pannier strapped to the side. You tell them to open it. Inside there is a pair of handcuffs, a map and 200 Credits. You handcuff the bikers to their own bike and look at the map. There is a red circle drawn around New Hope. Obviously these men come from the same gang that attacked New Hope. A small town named Rockville is marked with a red cross and is not far south-east from where you are now. No doubt it is the temporary home of the bikers. You decide to leave the bikers for their friends to find, and change the damaged wheel on the Interceptor (turn to **346**).

123

You are driving too fast to be able to swerve around the E-type. The Interceptor goes into an uncontroll-able spin and rolls over. Unfortunately it comes to rest on its roof. Suspended upside down by your seat-belt, you see several pairs of feet approaching the car. Leonardi and his friends dispense with formalities and drag you out of your car. They tie you up and leave you for the vultures. You watch helplessly as they set the Interceptor on fire. You have failed in your mission.

124

You are soon back at the T-junction and stop to decide which way to head. If you wish to turn right, turn to **203**. If you would rather turn left to head west, turn to **344**.

125

You spring up and leap at the guard. In the eerie half-light, you see a barely visible look of surprise on his face. You have the initiative and the chance to silence him before he raises the alarm. Roll two dice. If the total is the same as or less than your SKILL, turn to **349**. If the total is greater than your SKILL, turn to **202**.

126

You run across the road and press yourself against the wall of the building, half expecting another shot to ring out. Your heart beats fast as you creep forward slowly to the corner of the building and look round. There is nobody in sight down the narrow street. You take one step around the corner and then a voice shouts out, 'OK, that's far enough. One more step and you'll be full of holes. Where are you from?' If you reply that you are from New Hope, turn to **274**. If you reply that you are a lone road warrior, living nowhere in particular, turn to **155**.

127

You press the release button on the dashboard and watch the canister bounce along the road behind you. It suddenly bursts open, scattering the pointed iron spikes all over the road. Roll one die. If you roll between 1 and 4, turn to **373**. If you roll 5 or 6, turn to **220**.

128

Just as you are beginning to enjoy the freedom of the open road in the early-morning light, you are suddenly startled by the sight in your rearview-mirror of a vehicle closing up on you. It is an armoured car and you see a jet of flame flash from its gun barrel as a shell is fired at you. It explodes to your left, rocking the car, but you are able to keep control. Will you:

Drop iron spikes?	Turn to **312**
Release an oil spray?	Turn to **165**
Carry out a high-speed handbrake turn and face the armoured car?	Turn to **77**

129

Suddenly there is a deafening explosion, and the Interceptor is blown sideways by the force of a detonated mine. Roll two dice and deduct the total from the Interceptor's ARMOUR. If you survive the explosion, turn to **93**.

130

You steer the Interceptor round a sharp bend and are suddenly aware of an ominous rumbling sound. Stones fall on to the road in front of you, quickly followed by a shower of small boulders. It is difficult to look up the side of the canyon through your narrow windscreen, but you are only too aware that a landslide is beginning. If you wish to brake hard in the hope that the rocks and boulders will fall in front of you, turn to **314**. If you think it better to accelerate quickly away, turn to **71**.

131

You search through the dead man's pockets and find 150 Credits and a pair of knuckle-dusters. You pocket your findings and, when you feel strong enough, limp back to your Interceptor, wondering how long your Med-Kit will last. You turn the ignition key and burn up the road, heading east (turn to **22**).

132

You just beat your opponent to the draw, and watch him drop to the ground as your bullet finds its mark. You climb back inside the driver's cabin and set off north. All day you drive as fast as the tanker will go. Apart from a disorganized ambush attempt in the late afternoon, which you easily smash through with the armoured tanker, there are no incidents on the road. It is nearly dusk when you reach the outskirts of New Hope, its high, defended walls a strange but welcoming sight. If you were bitten by a rat on your homeward journey, turn to **275**. If you escaped being bitten, turn to **380**.

133

You are unable to control the speeding Interceptor and crash into the truck. Roll two dice and deduct the total from your car's ARMOUR score. If you survive the crash, turn to **151**.

134

If you still wish to drive back to the road to head south, turn to **207**. If you would rather take up the challenge of the Blitz Race after all, turn to **330**.

135

As the flames die down, you watch the bandit circle the car slowly. He calls out to you, making insults and derisory comments. His only weapon appears to be a dagger, which he is holding in his right hand. Trapped inside the car, you have no option but to climb out and confront the man. You draw your gun and open the door. As you step out, he immediately throws his dagger at you. Roll two dice. If the total is the same as or less than your SKILL, turn to **193**. If the total is greater than your SKILL, turn to **36**.

136

Amber curses and then bursts out laughing. The tube of energy pills that she was carrying has fallen out through a hole in her pocket. Turn to **32**.

137

You swerve sharply to the left, narrowly missing the stone pillar, and pass under the bridge. If you wish to stop to deal with your attacker, turn to **281**. If you would rather keep driving south, turn to **150**.

138

You stagger back from the thug as he slumps to the floor; just then the girl starts up the engine of the hot-rod. In a cloud of burning rubber she screeches

up the road on to the highway and is gone. If you wish to chase her, turn to **75**. If you would rather search the garage, turn to **146**.

139

The Ford slows down for a bend in the road, but you keep your foot down hard on the accelerator. You crash into the back of the Ford, but only succeed in damaging the Interceptor. Lose 2 ARMOUR points. The Ford has steel-plated crash bars built to with-stand ramming. You realize that you will have to overtake the Ford in order to use your rear missile weapons. As though he has read your mind, the Ford's driver starts to swing the car from side to side to stop you passing. It will take considerable man-oeuvring skill to pass him. Roll two dice. If the total is the same as or less than your SKILL, turn to **8**. If the total is greater than your SKILL, turn to **287**.

140

You travel about eighty kilometres before the road ends at a T-junction. You decide to turn right in the direction of San Anglo (turn to **23**).

141

You settle down to relax in the shade, while Pete busily sets to work on the engine. He taps and bangs away, whistling happily; you drift in and out of light sleep. Two hours later, he slams down the rein-forced engine cover and says, 'OK, she's ready to roll.' After giving Pete the 100 Credits and two packs of medical supplies, you start up the Interceptor and accelerate away as fast as possible. You can feel the extra acceleration in your back, and smile contentedly. Pete has done a good job. Add 1 LUCK point and turn to **88**.

142

You screech to a halt, but leave your engine running. Through your loudspeaker, you tell the man to raise his arms into the air and not to try any tricks. You notice that his motor bike is lying on its side just off the road. With your gun drawn, you carefully step out of the car. Suddenly the man in denim runs off the road and dives into the ditch just as something flies through the air and bounces on to the road between you and the Interceptor. With horror you see that it is a grenade. You see a blinding flash and in the same instant a deafening explosion knocks you off your feet. *Test your Luck*. If you are Lucky, turn to **299**. If you are Unlucky, turn to **25**.

143

Fearing that the two bikers might be part of a gang, you drive off south straight away in case the other members appear (turn to **96**).

144

Your headlights cut a white path through the night. On several occasions you have to swerve around abandoned cars and, as the night draws on, fatigue makes concentration very difficult. Roll two dice. If the total is the same or less than your SKILL, turn to **68**. If the total is greater than your SKILL, turn to **168**.

145

One of the gang sitting by the camp-fire has a sudden desire to sit in his beloved car. He stands up and walks over to the compound – and spots you crouching down by the fence. He calls out to his friends, saying, 'Hey, guess what, everybody – we've got visitors!' Pointing his rifle at you, he tells you to stand up and put your hands in the air. Within seconds you are surrounded by ten Doom Dogs, each one holding a gun. Your fate rests with this gang of desert outlaws, your mission a certain failure.

146

Everything inside the garage is either broken or useless. The office and workshop are filled with rubbish and a thick layer of dust covers everything. The man and the girl must just use the place occasionally as a trap for unwary passers-by. The only item you find that might be of use is a heavy chain. You coil it up and pack it inside the Interceptor before driving off on to the highway (turn to **167**).

147

You shout at the citizens to fall back and take cover inside the cabins. They obey your command and the battle commences. Suddenly, one of the Doom Dogs runs out from behind cover towards the armoured petrol tanker which has been prepared for you to drive back to New Hope. You shoot at him, but miss, and watch him open the driver's door. You have no choice but to run through the crossfire to stop him driving the tanker away. *Test your Luck*. If you are Lucky, turn to **235**. If you are Unlucky, turn to **279**.

148

You stamp down on the accelerator and release the clutch at the same time. The back wheels spin, but do not gain any traction. By the time you are moving, the Ford is already way ahead. Lose 1 LUCK point. Suddenly the Ford brakes hard and you race by it into the lead. In your rearview-mirror you watch the Ford accelerating quickly towards you. It must be supercharged. There is nothing you can do to stop being rammed. *Test your Luck*. If you are Lucky, turn to **354**. If you are Unlucky, turn to **247**.

149

The country road runs straight ahead far into the distance and you are able to make good headway, as it is relatively free from abandoned cars. After an hour's driving at high speed you arrive at a T-junction. If you wish to continue driving south, turn to **225**. If you wish to turn left and head east, turn to **114**.

150

It is not long before the green vegetation gives way to more barren terrain, with tufts of dry grass dotted on top of the stony, brown earth. You are soon at a major intersection on the edge of the desert. You stop at the crossroads and see that the road heading east is blocked with abandoned cars. If you wish to drive south into the desert, turn to 46. If you wish to turn right to head west, turn to 298.

151

You drive off the bridge, heading west again. You soon come to a T-junction which offers you a choice of roads. If you wish to keep driving west, turn to 179. If you would rather drive south, turn to 362.

152

You slam on the brakes and screech to a halt. The Ford crashes into your rear bumpers as the grenade explodes harmlessly in front of you. The ram, however, causes 2 points of damage to your ARMOUR. You accelerate and then brake again suddenly. The Ford swerves around you and accelerates away. As you are not allowed to use your forward-firing weapons, you decide to try to ram the Ford (turn to 139).

153

You continue to make good headway along the country roads. The untended fields on both sides of the road have grown wild, and you wonder how long it will be before they are farmed again. The road soon ends at a T-junction and you decide to turn left to head south towards San Anglo (turn to **225**).

154

Amber silences her two opponents, but you do not realize that you were being watched during your fight with the Doom Dogs. A fifth person remained inside the station-wagon – the Animal! On seeing the last of his gang fall to the ground, he leaps out of the station-wagon and runs at you unarmed, snorting like an angry bull. He is a terrifying sight in the moonlight. Huge and bare-chested, he wears a tight-fitting black face-mask, knee-high boots with steel toecaps, and his clenched fists are wrapped in studded leather. Before you have time to react, he wraps his arms around you in a bear hug and starts to squeeze. Lose 2 STAMINA points. Amber dares not risk shooting in case she hits you, and she looks around frantically for a hand-weapon. She grabs a spanner from the back of the car and runs to your aid. Roll 1 die. If you roll 1 or 2, turn to **245**. If you roll between 3 and 6, turn to **376**.

155

A man suddenly appears out of a doorway and walks towards you with his shotgun pointed at you. He looks at you sternly and says, 'You look like the person who shot up my station-wagon, killing my wife and son last week. Now I'll have my revenge – only I fight fair. Draw whenever you are ready.' You realize that it was a mistake to lie to the man. Lose 1 LUCK point. If you wish to try to talk your way out of the problem, turn to **219**. If you would rather draw your gun, turn to **333**.

156

'I thought that's what you said, but it's just that I've never heard of them before. I hope they aren't all as good at racing as you are. I expect I'll see you again – I'm going to join the others now,' says the tattooed man. Much to your relief he walks away, leaving you to drive off down the rough road to the main road where you turn right to head south (turn to **207**).

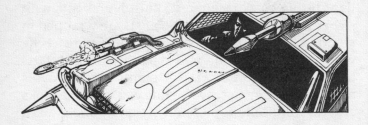

157

The dirt track is rough and bumpy, and you realize that people for miles around will see the dust that the speeding Interceptor is throwing up. Nevertheless, you are determined to reach Rockville. Suddenly, you see a blinding flash on top of a boulder in the distance. *Test your Luck*. If you are Lucky, turn to **222**. If you are Unlucky, turn to **315**.

158

You start up the Interceptor and turn to face your attackers. Your headlights illuminate a customized station-wagon which has thick sheets of plate steel riveted to its body and a pointed ramming bar protruding from its front grill. Machine-gun nozzles housed on either side of the ram bar suddenly open fire.

STATION-
  WAGON   FIREPOWER 10   ARMOUR 19

You are too close to the station-wagon to be able to launch a rocket, even if you have one left, and must return fire with your own machine-guns. If you survive three Attack Rounds of Vehicle Combat, turn to **67**.

159

Before too long you are back at the bridge which crosses the highway. You continue east along the road (turn to **341**).

160

The guard hears the noise caused by the rolling stone and looks down in your direction. He is only a few metres above you. If you wish to jump up and try to silence him before he raises the alarm, turn to **293**. If you would rather keep still on the ground, turn to **367**.

161

You shake your head and concentrate hard on your driving. After nearly falling asleep at the wheel several times during the night, your weariness departs as the first rays of morning sunlight creep over the horizon. You drive on south towards San Anglo with renewed enthusiasm (turn to **128**).

162

You see the look of surprise on Leonardi's face as you attempt to swerve round his parked car. Roll two dice. If the total is the same as or less than your SKILL, turn to **94**. If the total is greater than your SKILL, turn to **123**.

163

You are soon driving at high speed, until you arrive at a signpost which points down a narrow dirt track towards a town called Rockville. If you wish to drive south to Rockville, turn to **157**. If you would rather keep heading east, turn to **45**.

164

The hijacker tells you to step down on the road and prepare to draw your revolver. You jump down from the cabin and face the fearsome-looking man. With his crossbow pointed at the ground, he snarls loudly in order to unnerve you. But you are unperturbed by his tactics, and tell him to fire whenever he is ready. His arm comes up quickly to signal the start of the duel. Roll 1 die and add the number to your current SKILL score. Roll the die again and add the number to the hijacker's SKILL of 7. If your total is the same as or greater than that of the hijacker, turn to **132**. If the total is lower than that of the hijacker, turn to **205**.

165

You lean forward and press the button on the dashboard which releases the oil spray. The armoured car drives straight over the oil slick, and you watch with amusement as the driver struggles to control the skidding vehicle. Roll one die. If the number is between 1 and 5, turn to **234**. If the number rolled is 6, turn to **280**.

166

There is one wheel, in reasonable condition, remaining on the Interceptor. The tyre is flat but can easily be inflated again with the can of Flat-U-Fix. It does not take long to remove the wheel and store it inside your own car. If you wish to look inside the crashed car, turn to **253**. If you would rather continue your journey south, turn to **13**.

167

Despite the hazard of having to avoid abandoned cars, the highway is wide enough for you to gather plenty of speed. It's exciting to drive so freely, without fear of being hauled in by the police for violating some traffic regulation or other. You smile as your speed reaches 190 kilometres per hour, but your joy is shortlived: you suddenly see a red Chevrolet, heavily reinforced with steel plating, coming straight towards you. Somebody is sitting in a small turret on the roof – a machine-gunner. You think to yourself that maybe having to deal with the police in the old days wasn't so bad compared with what is coming at you now. You breathe in deeply and get ready to press the machine-gun fire button.

RED CHEVVY   FIREPOWER 8   ARMOUR 15

If you manage to destroy the Chevvy in this Vehicle Combat, turn to **188**.

168

Late in the night, your tiredness slows down your reactions. A bus appears in your headlights, and you swerve too late to avoid hitting it. Roll two dice and deduct the total from the Interceptor's ARMOUR. If you survive the crash, turn to **327**.

169

The man works for an hour, welding on extra steel panels and patching up holes where he can. The Interceptor looks in a very sorry state, but at least it is better protected. Add 10 ARMOUR points. You thank the man for his work, pay him, and set off east again (turn to **259**).

170

The man does not notice what you are doing and you manage to slip the knuckle-dusters on to your fingers. You spin round and swing your fist at the man's face. Roll two dice. If the total is the same as or less than your SKILL, turn to **363**. If the total is greater than your SKILL, turn to **87**.

171

Luckily, none of the stray bullets hits you. You wonder how long your Med-Kit is going to last if the mission is going to continue being so dangerous. When you finally feel strong enough to drive, you limp over to the Interceptor and burn up the road, heading east (turn to **22**).

172

Miraculously, you manage to drive swiftly through the falling rocks and boulders without being hit. You breathe a sigh of relief when you are clear of the landslide, and slow down to a safer speed for negotiating the winding road (turn to **351**).

173

A second shell is fired from the farmhouse with devastating effect against your damaged Interceptor. You do not survive the explosion.

174

The man makes the mistake of aiming at your chest, unaware of your protection. The bullet does you no harm. You do not give him a second chance and fling open the door to pull him out of the driver's seat on to the ground. He is easily overcome, and then you order him to tell his friends to call off the attack. He reluctantly agrees to your demand and the shooting stops almost immediately. You keep your gun trained on your hostage while you watch the rest of the Doom Dogs retreat back into the desert. You let the captured Doom Dog follow his friends to the jeers and cheers of the inhabitants of the San Anglo refinery. After helping with the repairs to the entrance, you tell them that it is time for you to leave. You climb into the cabin of the tanker and wave farewell. You feel sad to be abandoning your faithful Interceptor, but realize the importance of this mission. Two cars escort you north along the road until you reach the edge of the desert. Then they turn and drive back to San Anglo, leaving you alone on the highway once more. You decide to head directly north, ignoring all turnings that you come to. The day passes without incident and you keep on driving well into the night. When you are too tired to drive any further, you pull into a motel car-park, as there are no lights showing in the rooms. If you wish to sleep inside the cabin of the tanker, turn to **218**. If you wish to go inside the motel, turn to **335**.

175

The grenade fails to explode and you are left racing ahead of the yellow car by some fifty metres (turn to **340**).

176

Roll two dice. If the total is the same as or less than your SKILL score, turn to **108**. If the total is higher than your SKILL score, turn to **350**.

177

You drive along the edge of the desert for about eighty kilometres until you arrive at a major intersection. The road ahead is blocked with abandoned cars so you decide to turn right to head south again (turn to **46**).

178

You frantically turn the ignition key and pump the accelerator, but the engine will not start. You look inside the engine compartment and notice that the fuel pipe has come away from the carburettor. You twist it back on and are about to climb back into the car when you suddenly feel a tickling sensation down your spine. You whirl round and see a man standing motionless, feet slightly apart, pointing a large-bore hand-gun at you, possibly an old Magnum. He is dressed as a cowboy with boots, stetson hat and even a cigar in his mouth. In a low voice he growls, 'Draw!'

OUTLAW   SKILL 9   STAMINA 12

Resolve this combat using the Shooting rules, but reduce your SKILL by 2 for the first Attack Round as the outlaw has the initiative. If you win, turn to **375**, but reduce your SKILL permanently by 1 point if you are shot more than once.

179

Standing in the middle of the road, waving his arms frantically, is a man wearing denim jeans and jacket. A motor-cycle helmet covers his head. If you wish to stop to talk to him, turn to **142**. If you would rather drive past him, turn to **215**.

180

You stop the car and pour the contents of the can into the petrol tank. You know that you do not have enough fuel to reach San Anglo and wonder where you will find some more in this desert wilderness. It is a depressing thought, which weighs on your mind as you set off again (turn to **243**).

181

You watch with satisfaction as the front tyres of the armoured car are shredded by the spikes, forcing the driver to brake hard. You accelerate away, leaving behind the stranded armoured car (turn to **47**).

182

You crawl painfully into the tall grass and wait. Soon you hear the noise of approaching footsteps. Through the grass you see a scruffy man, gun in hand, standing only a few metres away. A cigar hangs out of the corner of his mouth and around his head is tied a red headband. He is obviously the man who set the booby-trap. Suddenly he sees your trail of blood leading into the grass. He turns and fires blindly into the grass. *Test your Luck*. If you are Lucky, turn to **227**. If you are Unlucky, turn to **116**.

183

The Ford driver is anticipating your breakaway, and calmly presses the button of the grenade-launcher. The grenade flies over the Interceptor and bounces along the road in front of you. Will you accelerate over it (turn to **43**) or brake hard (turn to **152**)?

184

The Doom Dogs are too enraged to care about their word of honour. They draw their weapons, and a shoot-out begins. You take on two of them while Amber returns fire at the other two.

	SKILL	STAMINA
First DOOM DOG	7	13
Second DOOM DOG	8	14

During this Shooting combat, both Doom Dogs will fire separately at you during each Attack Round, but you must choose which of the two you will fire at. Against the other you will throw for your Attack Strength in the normal way, but you will not wound him if your Attack Strength is greater – you must just count this as though you dodged his bullet. Of course, if his Attack Strength is greater, he will wound you in the normal way. If you win, turn to **69**, but reduce your SKILL permanently by 1 point if you are shot more than once during the shoot-out.

185

The door opens into a room that has recently been occupied. There are unfinished cups of coffee on the table and the front wheel of a motor cycle propped up against the wall, its inner tube lying on the floor. Somebody was obviously in the process of mending a puncture. There is also a tool-kit on the table, inside which you find a pair of heavy-duty wire-cutters which you decide to take with you. If you have not done so already, you may open the door to the room opposite (turn to **72**); or you may leave the house (turn to **246**).

186

Yawning almost constantly, you try to concentrate on driving down the straight country road; but after the efforts of the day, fatigue makes you fall asleep at the wheel. You drive straight into the back of an abandoned truck which is half blocking the road. Roll two dice and deduct the total from the Interceptor's ARMOUR. If you survive the crash, turn to **348**.

187

You do not have anything with which to siphon the petrol out of the tank, and have no alternative but to carry on south (turn to **118**).

188

You stop your Interceptor to examine the burning wreck. Who were these people and why did they attack you without warning? You shake your head and hit the accelerator, eager to reach your destination. You are passing a security truck and thinking about all the money inside it which is now useless, when suddenly a voice comes through on your radio above the crackling static. It is one of New Hope's leaders. She tells you how a gang of bikers have just attacked New Hope, killing eight people in the process. After a short battle, they were eventually beaten off. She warns you to be on the lookout for them, as they have kidnapped Sinclair, the council leader. You acknowledge the message and say goodbye. After an hour or so of driving without any further incident, you notice that your petrol gauge is dropping; the Interceptor is very heavy on petrol. You stop and pour the contents of the fuel canister into the tank, realizing that you will have to find some more petrol soon. A few kilometres further and you know your luck has really run out. There must have been a car crash at the time of the disaster which caused a huge tail-back of now-abandoned cars. It is impossible to continue along the highway. You reverse back to the last exit and drive off the highway. You must decide which way to head along the road which crosses over it. If you wish to drive east, turn to **341**. If you wish to drive west, turn to **66**.

189

Leading off the road on your right is a rough road which is marked with several sets of tyre tracks. The tracks look as if they were made quite recently. If you wish to drive down the rough road, turn to **24**. If you would rather stay on course for San Anglo, turn to **207**.

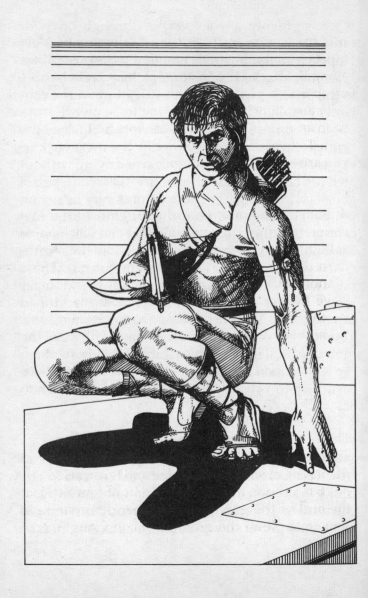

190

It is frustrating just to sit inside the tanker. All is quiet until you hear the sound of footsteps walking along the top of the trailer. The hijacker intends to creep up on you from behind. You open the cabin door and climb up the metal ladder to meet him. As soon as your head appears, he fires his crossbow at you. *Test your Luck*. If you are Lucky, turn to **345**. If you are Unlucky, turn to **30**.

191

A bullet punctures one of your front tyres. You momentarily lose control of the car and hit a boulder at high speed. Roll one die and deduct the number from the car's ARMOUR for the crash damage. You cannot drive on the flat tyre, but it is dangerous to leave the car while under fire. Suddenly you see another blinding flash; the bazooka is being fired through a top-floor window of the farmhouse. You are a sitting target and the shell does not miss. Roll two dice and deduct the total from your car's ARMOUR. If you survive the explosion, turn to **292**.

192

The tattooed man does not fall for the trick, and easily sidesteps your attempted karate kick. He points the machine-gun at you and tells you to walk on, but as soon as you are in front of him he slams the butt of the gun against the back of your head. You crumple to the ground, unconscious (turn to **100**).

193

You duck down behind the car door and the dagger bounces harmlessly off it. From out of a shoulder-holster the man pulls a small revolver ready for the shoot-out.

BANDIT   SKILL 7   STAMINA 11

Resolve this combat using the Shooting rules, but add 1 point to your own SKILL for the duration of the battle because of your cover behind the car door. If you win, turn to **64**, but reduce your SKILL permanently by 1 point if you are shot more than once.

194

Both dune buggies are ablaze; you decide to get away as quickly as possible. Eighty kilometres further south, you see a range of flat-topped hills rising out of the desert sand directly ahead. The road finally ends at the foot of these hills. Looking left and right, you see the road run straight as an arrow east to west. If you wish to turn left, turn to **257**. If you wish to turn right, turn to **211**.

195

You turn the handle and pull. An explosion, accompanied by a brilliant white flash and deafening noise, sends you reeling backwards. The door was booby-trapped! Roll 1 die and deduct the number from your STAMINA score. The door hangs off its hinges but there is nothing inside the ambulance. Its owner will probably be on his way now to see who he has caught. You feel too weak to reach the Interceptor, and decide to crawl into hiding. If you wish to hide in the grass, turn to **182**. If you wish to hide under the ambulance, turn to **356**.

196

Heeding the man's advice, you keep a wary eye out for falling rocks and drive through the canyon very slowly. Suddenly you hear an ominous rumbling sound ahead. You steer round a sharp bend and see a landslide in progress, with rocks and boulders crashing down on to the road. It soon stops, and you are able to continue, as the road is not completely blocked (turn to **351**).

197

You stop the car and get out to empty the fuel canister into the petrol tank. The canister does not hold much petrol and you realize that you will have to be on the look-out for more, if you hope to reach San Anglo. By the time you set off again it is early evening and you watch the setting sun through the right-hand window. Soon it will be dark and there is a new decision to make. Will you:

Drive off the road and sleep inside the Interceptor?	Turn to **4**
Find a building to spend the night inside?	Turn to **321**
Drive on through the night?	Turn to **144**

198

You reach the barbed-wire fence and see eight vehicles inside its perimeter. The coiled wire is too finely meshed for you to be able to squeeze through without becoming entangled. If you possess a pair of wire-cutters, turn to **85**. If you do not, turn to **255**.

199

The farmhouse is an easy target and the rocket does not miss. The explosion destroys the farmhouse, sending fragments of brick and wood flying through the air. When the dust has settled, you

drive cautiously ahead, one finger against the machine-gun trigger. You stop alongside the burning farmhouse, but see no signs of life. You turn off the engine and wind down the window of the Interceptor. You hear the desperate cry of a man calling for help. If you wish to get out of the car to investigate, turn to **262**. If you would rather drive south out of town, turn to **353**.

200

You manage to avoid a head-on collision, but are rammed in the side by the station-wagon. Its pointed ram bar pierces the Interceptor's reinforced panel, locking the two vehicles together. The station-wagon's loudspeaker immediately barks out a message from the Animal – fight him hand to hand or shoot it out. If you wish to fight the Animal, turn to **269**. If you wish to shoot it out, turn to **102**.

201

Suddenly there is a dull thud, and the Interceptor rocks from side to side. Roll two dice and deduct the total from the Interceptor's ARMOUR. If you survive the explosion, turn to **266**.

202

Although you knock the guard to the ground, he remains conscious, and calls out to his friends. They all leap up and run over to where you are fighting. Amber shouts at you to run down the hill to escape. But before there is time to do anything, you are mown down by a hail of bullets. Your adventure is over.

203

The road is open and wrecked cars are an infrequent hazard. The speedometer reads well above the maximum speed-limit that used to control the road, but you know that there is no chance of getting a speeding-ticket now. Your enjoyment, however, is short lived: a road-block of upturned cars and trucks comes into view. You slow down and survey the scene, sensing danger. Will you:

Fire a rocket at the road-block?	Turn to **372**
Try to drive around the road-block?	Turn to **317**
Turn around and drive back to the last junction to head south?	Turn to **278**

204

The bullets miss you and you start the engine without delay. In a cloud of dust you screech away down the rough road to the highway, where you turn right at speed to head south (turn to 207).

205

Your opponent is quicker to the draw than you are. He fires the crossbow bolt with deadly accuracy, into the middle of your chest. You sink to the ground, firing your gun wildly. Your adventure ends here.

206

You fire at the lock on the pannier. Three shots and it's open. Inside you find a pair of handcuffs, a map and 200 Credits. After putting the handcuffs and Credits in your jacket pocket, you look at the map. There is a red circle drawn around New Hope. Obviously these men came from the same gang that attacked New Hope. A small town named Rockville is marked with a red cross and is not too far southeast from where you are now. No doubt it is the temporary home of the bikers. You decide to change the wheel on your Interceptor before any of the bikers' friends arrive (turn to 346).

207

You flash past a handwritten sign which reads 'Pete makes engines sweet. One mile to the left.' You slow down as you approach a stone building with a corrugated iron workshop attached to it which has the words 'Spark Plug Pete's' painted on a billboard on top of the roof. There are a few cars parked on the forecourt. As you come to a halt, a thin pale man appears from the workshop wearing an oily blue mechanic's overall and a baseball cap. He waves and says, 'Nice car. Pretty fast, I guess. But not as fast as old Pete can make it. If you are interested, I like payment in Credits and goods. I'll do a good job for you.' If you wish to stop to let the mechanic modify your engine, turn to **28**. If you would rather refuse his offer politely and continue your journey south, turn to **88**.

208

The man tells you that it has been an honour fighting you in such a civilized manner. He goes on to say that, after the road has passed through the tunnel, it then winds through a twisting canyon and you should be on the look-out for landslides. You thank the strange man for his advice and drive into the tunnel, once he has reversed the bus out of the way. Sure enough, you find yourself driving along the winding road through the canyon (turn to **196**).

209

As you hand the keys to the thug, he merely sniggers and lunges at you with his crowbar. You are

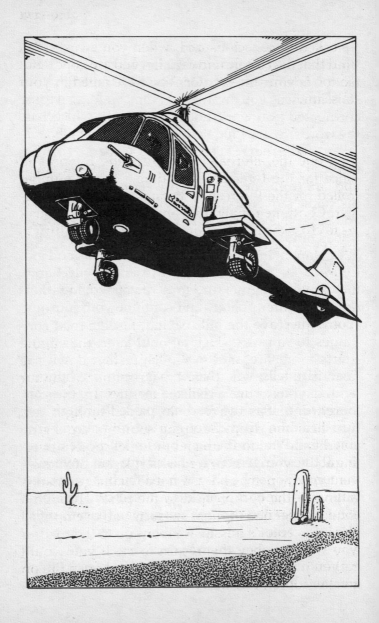

knocked unconscious and, when you awake, you find that the couple and their hot-rod are gone – but so too is your Interceptor. You have failed in your mission.

210

Roll one die alternately, once for the E-type and once for the Interceptor, adding 1 to the number rolled for the Interceptor because of its supercharger. Continue rolling until one car reaches a total of 24 to cross the finishing-line first. If you win, turn to **54**. If you lose the race, turn to **322**.

211

You soon leave the hills behind, but the road continues to run west. Half an hour later, the engine starts to misfire, and not much further down the road it cuts out completely. You get out of the car and diagnose the problem as sand in the carburettor. Just as you have finished cleaning it out, you hear the deep thumping sound of an engine overhead. You look up and see a helicopter hovering above you. It is covered with splashes of fluorescent yellow paint and you notice that a gunman is sitting in the cockpit next to the pilot. Through a loudspeaker one of them instructs you to empty all the Interceptor's missile weapons on to the road. If you wish to obey them, turn to **11**. If you would rather jump inside the Interceptor and open fire on the helicopter, turn to **83**.

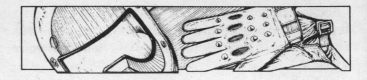

212

The car slides to a halt in a cloud of dust, and you jump out firing your revolver. The two bikers return fire as you scramble away from the Interceptor before the mine explodes. You dive on to the ground to hide behind a bush, just as the explosion rips through the air, wrecking a wheel. Lose 2 ARMOUR points. The dust settles and all is silent, until one of the bikers calls out to you, saying, 'Throw out your gun and keys. We only want your car.' If you wish to obey them, turn to **283**. If you would rather fight it out, turn to **6**.

213

The oil sinks into the dirt-covered road and has no effect on the car behind. Lose 1 LUCK point. The driver of the Ford retaliates by firing a grenade over your car to land on the road in front of you. There is a muffled explosion as the steel-plated underchassis takes the full blast of the grenade. Roll two dice and deduct the total from your car's ARMOUR. If you survive the explosion, turn to **294**.

214

As you approach the group under the trees, you realize that you will have to try and make a run for it. You pretend to stumble and then suddenly kick your leg out sideways at the tattooed man. Roll one die. If you roll between 1 and 4, turn to **192**. If you roll 5 or 6, turn to **347**.

215

You travel west looking for a major road going south. But the decision is made for you when you arrive at a solid tail-back of cars just beyond a left turning. The impassable blockade of cars and trucks stretches into the distance as far as you can see, all of them long since abandoned. If you wish to head south, turn to **149**. If you would rather stop and look inside some of the abandoned vehicles, turn to **10**.

216

The road eventually ends at a T-junction and you are able to turn left to head south once again (turn to **243**).

217

The man appears unperturbed as you run towards him. He continues to chant about cleansing the earth and ridding the world of all traces of the decadent past. You reach him just as he is about to throw the lighted match on to the Interceptor. Roll two dice. If the total is the same as or less than your SKILL, turn to **285**. If the total is higher than your SKILL, turn to **50**.

218

Although you sleep very lightly, waking at the slightest sound, the night passes peacefully. At first light you are on the road again. All is fine for an hour or so, until you see in your wing mirror two motor bikes approaching. Unfortunately the petrol tanker is not armed with rear missile weapons, but it has a swivel-mounted machine-gun on the cabin roof. As they draw nearer, you see that both bikers are carrying crossbows. They accelerate alongside the tanker, one on each side, and fire their crossbows at your front tyres. You reply by firing your machine-gun at the bike on your left. Roll two dice. If the total is the same as or less than your SKILL, turn to **52**. If the total is greater than your SKILL, turn to **324**.

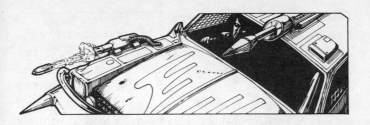

219

You tell him quickly that you did not kill his wife and son. *Test your Luck*. If you are Lucky, turn to **288**. If you are Unlucky, turn to **236**.

220

The motor-bike rider somehow manages to steer the vehicle around the spikes and the passenger opens fire at you again. You decide to return fire with the Interceptor's machine-gun, although the swerving target is difficult to hit.

MOTOR BIKE
  and SIDECAR   FIREPOWER 9   ARMOUR 8

If you win this highway battle, turn to **143**.

The road cuts a straight black line through the nightmare-red landscape. The desert heat rises from the sand in shimmering waves and your air-conditioner rattles in its noisy struggle to keep you cool. Your radio picks up nothing but static and crackles away monotonously. You keep the accelerator pressed to the floor as you speed through the badlands. Ahead in the distance you see black smoke curling up into the air. You slow down and brake alongside a burning car. It's an old sports car from the last century; a Corvette with its 200 brake horsepower V8 engine. A beast of the past abruptly ending its life in a ball of fire. Leaning casually against a boulder away from the burning wreck is a blonde woman, wearing black overalls and holding a shotgun. When she sees the Interceptor approach, she runs out into the road to wave you down. You stop in front of her, your hand reaching for your revolver in case she tries to hijack the Interceptor. You ask her where she is going, and in a stern voice she replies, 'South, as far as you are concerned. I just want a lift – unless you also belong to that wild gang of road warriors who attacked me.' You tell her that you are on a mission to San Anglo and offer her a ride. 'San Anglo!' she yells. 'You must be the person we have been expecting from New Hope!' She jumps in the car and introduces herself as Amber. She says that a message went out to all patrol vehicles to be on the look-out for the Interceptor, but she had to be sure that you were who you said you were. She also tells you that there is a complication. For the last two days, San Anglo has been under constant attack from a large gang of road warriors known as the Doom Dogs, led by a man they call the Animal. It was the Doom Dogs who attacked her, less than an hour ago. They are determined to massacre the inhabitants of San Anglo to have access to the reserves of petrol. It is now virtually impossible to leave or enter San Anglo without being attacked by their heavily armed cars and motor bikes. There is only one solution – to break into their camp at night and sabotage their vehicles. The look of determination in Amber's eyes convinces you that there is no alternative, and you agree to help her. She slaps the dashboard in eager excitement and tells you to drive south as quickly as possible. Half an hour later, Amber tells you to stop. In the distance, you can see smoke rising into the air. 'San Anglo refinery,' she says in a proud voice. 'We'd rather die than let the vermin steal the petrol from us. Turn left off the road. It will be dark in an hour and then we'll have to leave the car and walk to the Doom Dogs' camp.' *Test your Luck*. If you are Lucky, turn to 7. If you are Unlucky, turn to 331.

222
Somebody has fired a bazooka at you, but the shell explodes harmlessly a few metres to your left. Turn to 53.

223
You jack the car up and put on the spare wheel. A few minutes later you are driving east again, carefully trying to avoid sharp stones. You drive for an hour across the bumpy terrain, until you finally

reach another road running north to south. You turn right on to it, grateful to be driving on a smooth road again. You pass an articulated truck which looks as if it has only recently been parked. If you wish to stop and examine the truck, turn to 104. If you would rather drive on without stopping, turn to 118.

224

The first race is between a yellow Ford and a red Porsche; they race off down the road, ramming each other and using their array of weapons. They return about six minutes later, the Ford winning by a couple of seconds. Both cars look like wrecks. The driver of the Ford leaps out of his car and begins cheering. While he is still enjoying his victory, you walk back to the Interceptor to drive back to the main road to head south again (turn to 207).

225

The road cuts through overgrown fields, but there are no obstructions on the road. You check your milometer to see how far you have come, and see that the petrol gauge is reading empty again. If you have picked up a full fuel canister recently, turn to 197. If you have not picked one up, turn to 364.

226

Your attacker is well trained in the art of wrestling. With one dextrous manoeuvre he flips you on to your back and then pushes you off the top of the trailer. You land heavily on the road below and are knocked unconscious. You wake some time later, but the petrol tanker is gone. You have failed in your mission.

227

The bullet thuds into the ground only a metre away. You immediately sit up and return fire.

HIGHWAYMAN   SKILL 8   STAMINA 12

Resolve this combat using the Shooting rules, but reduce your SKILL by 1 point for the duration of the fight because of your injury. If you win, turn to **131**, but reduce your SKILL permanently by 1 point if you are shot more than once.

228

'Liar! I didn't think you looked like a member of a gang. Let's hear what the others have to say about this.' He waves his machine-gun in the direction of the trees where his friends are sitting. If you possess a pair of knuckle-dusters, turn to **273**. If you do not have them, turn to **214**.

229

You crawl on to the bridge, steering carefully to avoid the wheels coming off the two main beams. Suddenly there is a loud explosion. Somebody has detonated the bridge, sending the Interceptor crashing into the river below. You have failed in your mission.

230

Set back about thirty metres from the road is a small white building which is completely surrounded by cars in various stages of assembly. Wheels, doors, bumpers, axles, engines, gearboxes and seats are strewn everywhere and, in the middle of it all, is a man working away at one car. He is busy using an oxy-acetylene torch on a door-panel, causing sparks to fly everywhere. He is so engrossed in his work that he doesn't hear you arrive. If you wish to talk to him about repairing the Interceptor, turn to 15. If you would rather drive on, turn to 259.

231

The front wheels slam down on the opposite side of the bridge, but the rear wheels just miss it. The car slides backwards and plunges thirty metres into the river below. You have failed in your mission.

232

The small group of spectators gathers around the Ford to congratulate the driver. You drive past him slowly, waving in salute of his victory, but do not stop. You are bitterly disappointed at losing the race and are keen to drive back to the main road to head south (turn to 207).

233

After attending to your wound, you find that there is nothing apart from rubbish and broken furniture in the room; it was merely booby-trapped to deter intruders. Lose 1 LUCK point. If you have not done so already, you may open the door of the room opposite (turn to **185**); or you may leave the house (turn to **246**).

234
The driver is unable to control the skidding armoured car, and it runs off the road into a ditch. You smile and accelerate away, leaving behind the immobilized vehicle (turn to **47**).

235
Keeping your head as low as possible, you run across the open space without being caught in the crossfire (turn to **40**).

236
The man looks at you and spits on the floor before saying, 'Draw, I said, you murdering scum!' You have no choice but to obey him (turn to **333**).

237
You manage to drive south only eight kilometres before the Interceptor becomes bogged down in soft sand. The wheels spin, sending clouds of sand into the air, but you only succeed in burying the Interceptor deeper. You curse your luck, but there is no hope of extracting the car from the soft sand without help. You try to dig it out, but it is a futile struggle, and you realize despondently that you will have to abandon the Interceptor. With luck you will make it back to New Hope and try to reach San Anglo again another time.

238

The tyre is not badly damaged and you are able to fix the puncture with the can of Flat-U-Fix. It is not long before you are driving east again (turn to **119**).

239

The Ford races ahead over the bridge as you press down on the accelerator again to try to catch up. You see the finishing-line ahead, no more than two hundred metres away, and realize that the race is lost. The Ford crosses the finishing line a car's length ahead of the Interceptor. Lose 1 LUCK point and turn to **232**.

240

You take 200 Credits out of your pocket and thrust them towards the man with the scar. He snatches them from you and says, 'There's a sucker born every minute. Get in your car. Let's do it. We race for eight kilometres down the dirt road, turn around at the white house, and race back. And remember, there are no holds barred in a Blitz Race, except bullets and rockets.' You climb inside the Interceptor, start it up and crawl forward to the starting-line. Your opponent draws alongside you in his bright yellow Ford. You see that it is armed with two machine-guns and a grenade-launcher. A girl standing in between the two cars raises a white towel into the air and then suddenly pulls it down to signal the start of the race. Roll two dice. If the total is the same as or less than your SKILL, turn to **3**. If the total is greater than your SKILL, turn to **148**.

241

Using an iron bar from the tanker's tool-box, you soon prise the motel door open. You walk cautiously into the reception area, where your nostrils are filled with a nauseating smell of rotting vegetation. You shine your torch around and see rubbish and filth strewn all over the floor. Swing doors open into the main hallway, and there is a staircase leading to the upper floor. As you survey the scene, you suddenly hear the sound of light footsteps above you. You shine the torch up the staircase and catch sight of a pair of feet. A sinewy old man dressed in tattered rags suddenly runs down the stairs holding a huge rat in each hand. 'This is the home of the rat man,' he shouts in a scratchy voice, 'and you will pay for your unwelcome visit!' Catching you off balance, he throws the two rats at you. They land on your chest and you try frantically to brush them off. You are bitten just once before you manage to get them off you. Lose 1 STAMINA point. The rat man laughs maniacally and runs back up the stairs. You decide that the motel is no place to spend the night and walk back to the tanker. You drive a few miles further up the road before finding somewhere else to park, and remain inside the cabin to sleep (turn to 218).

242

Neither of the tyres is too badly damaged, and you are able to inflate them with the can of Flat-U-Fix. It is not long before you are motoring east again (turn to 119).

243

On the right-hand side of the road, you see an abandoned police car, half-covered by a drift of sand. If you wish to stop to see if there is anything of use to you inside the car, turn to **109**. If you would rather keep driving south, turn to **49**.

244

Your injury slows down your reflexes, and your hand has only just reached the handle of your knife when the man fires three shots from his gun in quick succession. He does not miss from point-blank range, and you are dead before you hit the floor.

245

As Amber tries to strike the Animal with the spanner, he rolls on to the ground with you still locked in his vice-like grip. Lose 2 STAMINA points. Again Amber tries to strike the giant man. Roll 1 die. If you roll 1 or 2, turn to **360**. If you roll between 3 and 6, turn to **376**.

246

If you have not done so already, you may search the general store (turn to **112**). Otherwise there is nothing else to do except drive off south (turn to **353**).

247

The Interceptor swerves to the left, but you steer into the skid to keep the car under control. The Ford rams you again, this time doing some damage. Lose 2 ARMOUR points. In your mirror you see the Ford closing in again, and you have to think quickly to decide what tactics to use. Will you accelerate away (turn to **183**) or brake hard to let the Ford pass you (turn to **27**)?

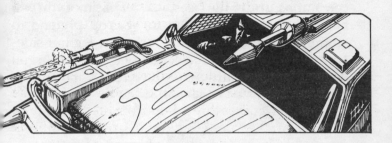

248

Your reactions are too slow and the driver's door receives the full impact of the high-speed ram. The pointed ram bar pierces the reinforced door, killing you instantly. Your adventure ends in the desert night.

249

You walk over to the wrecked bike, carrying your revolver in one hand and the Med-Kit in the other. One of the men is dead and the other is barely alive. You kick his pistol away from him and see if he can be saved. He opens his eyes, smiles and says, 'Fat Jack and the boys will get you for this.' Then he slumps back and is still. Your Med-Kit cannot help him. You check the bike over and notice a locked side-pannier. If you would like to open the pannier, turn to **206**. If you would rather head off east without wasting any more time, turn to **163**.

250

The man notices you putting your hand in your pocket and tells you to keep on walking with your hands on your head. As you approach the group celebrating under the trees, you realize that you will have to try to make a run for it. You pretend to stumble and then suddenly kick your leg out sideways at the tattooed man. Roll one die. If you roll between 1 and 4, turn to **192**. If you roll 5 or 6, turn to **347**.

251

You check your compass to make sure you are heading directly east. The Interceptor vibrates as it crosses the stony ground and suddenly you hear a loud bang. The Interceptor becomes difficult to steer, the obvious sign of a flat tyre. You stop to inspect the damage and find that the tyre has blown and cannot be inflated by Flat-U-Fix. If you are carrying a spare wheel, turn to **223**. If you do not have a spare wheel, turn to **343**.

252

You open the front door of the house and step inside. Leading off the hallway there are two doors facing each other. If you wish to open the door on the left, turn to **185**. If you wish to open the door on the right, turn to **72**.

253

You pull open the driver's door and reach inside to open the glove compartment. Suddenly you hear a rattling sound and realize with horror that you have disturbed the nest of a rattlesnake. The snake strikes and bites your arm, emptying deadly poison into your veins. If you still possess a pack of medicine from your Med-Kit, turn to **2**. If you have used up all the Med-Kit supplies, turn to **357**.

254

The countryside is picturesque in the early-morning light, but you are unaware of the dangers ahead. The road has been mined by country outlaws, waiting to rob anybody passing through. Roll one die. If you roll 1, 2 or 3, turn to **129**. If you roll 4, 5 or 6, turn to **101**.

255

You have no alternative but to crawl round the perimeter of the barbed-wire fence until you reach the entrance gate to the compound. *Test your Luck*. If you are Lucky, turn to **339**. If you are Unlucky, turn to **145**.

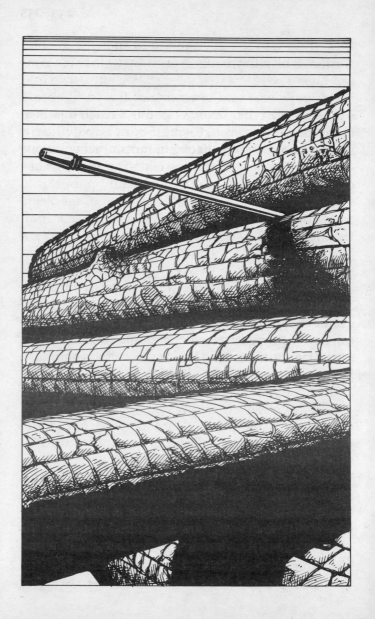

256

Although bleeding badly, you manage to reach your car. Lose 1 extra STAMINA point. You flop down into the driver's seat and open one of the packs inside the Med-Kit. Soon your wound is treated – pellets removed and a layer of synthi-skin applied, with bandages to cover it. Back behind the wheel, your spirit returns as you drop the clutch and screech out of town (turn to 34).

257

Up ahead you see that the road is blocked by a barricade made of logs taken from an abandoned truck. The long, thin barrel of some sort of weapon protrudes from the logs. You decide to stop and open the door of your car to negotiate with the gunner to let you drive around the barricade. You call out stating your request but the reply is curt and to the point. 'Go back. This is a car-free zone. You have been warned.' If you wish to heed the advice and turn around to head west, turn to 337. If you would rather ignore the advice and press on east, turn to 9.

258

You run out of the outhouse and grab your Med-Kit from the car. You use one pack of the medicine, but this does not restore any STAMINA points; it merely stops the poison from spreading further through your system. Not wishing to spend the rest of the night inside the outhouse, you must decide what to do. If you wish to sleep inside the car, turn to 297. If you wish to start your engine and drive on through the night, turn to **144**.

259

Ahead in the distance looms a range of hills. As you arrive at the foot of the hills you see that the road passes under them via a tunnel. Unfortunately there is a bus blocking the entrance. You stop the car and walk up to the bus to see whether or not it can be started and moved out of the way. The driver's door suddenly opens and a masked man jumps down on to the road pointing a gun at you. 'To pass through this tunnel you must either pay me a toll of 200 Credits or engage me in a pistol duel,' he says in a very matter-of-fact tone. If you wish to pay the toll, turn to **369**. If you fancy your chances at a pistol duel, turn to **291**.

260

You shout at the robed man, telling him to move away from your car. But he continues his chant which appears to be about cleansing the earth and ridding the world of all traces of the decadent past. Paying no attention to you, he drops the lighted match on to the Interceptor which is immediately engulfed in flames. Your anger is futile; the fanatic has put an end to your mission.

261

The back of the roof is squashed almost flat on to the rear seats, but the driver's section is left intact. The landslide is not heavy enough to block the road completely and you are able to continue as soon as the rocks stop falling (turn to 351).

262

You walk over towards the sound of the cry for help and find that it is coming from inside a shack attached to the general store. You ask who is inside the shack – it's Sinclair, New Hope's council leader! You search round and find an iron bar to prise open the lock on the door. Soon Sinclair is free. Add 1 LUCK point. Sinclair tells you about the raid on New Hope and his kidnapping. He asks you to radio to New Hope to tell them that he will return by motor bike as soon as possible. There are two bikes parked in front of the General Store, of which he chooses the old Harley Davidson. Thanking you for your help, he waves goodbye and roars off north. Will you:

Search the general store?	Turn to 112
Search the nearest house?	Turn to 252
Drive off south?	Turn to 353

263

The bullet hits you in the chest, killing you instantly. Your adventure comes to a sudden end.

264

Carrying the crowbar, you leap across the roofs of the cars to hurry back to the Interceptor. Luckily it is still where you left it and you are soon on the road again, heading south (turn to **149**).

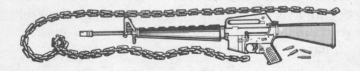

265

You do not stop in case some more of Leonardi's friends appear. You keep up the same fast pace for fifteen kilometres, until you pass an articulated truck which looks as if it has only recently been parked. If you wish to stop and examine the truck, turn to **104**. If you would rather drive on without stopping, turn to **118**.

266

The Ford races past you as you struggle to keep the damaged car going. As you are not allowed to use your forward-firing weapons, you decide to try to ram the Ford (turn to **139**).

267

You park your Interceptor and walk back to the ambulance. The driver's cab is empty, although the ambulance looks as if it has been driven quite recently. If you wish to open the rear door to look inside, turn to **195**. If you would rather get back inside the Interceptor and head east, turn to **22**.

268

Fortunately the engine was not damaged by the explosion and it starts up straight away. You drive off hastily, lucky to have survived (turn to **303**).

269

You shout out that you will accept the challenge to fight the Animal, on condition that you will be allowed to leave if you win. The Animal agrees to the terms. You watch two men and two women climb out of the station-wagon. They start to bang on the Interceptor with their guns, chanting their leader's name out loud: 'AN-I-MAL. AN-I-MAL. AN-I-MAL.'. The station-wagon's passenger door slowly opens, and a huge, bare-chested man steps out wearing a tight-fitting face-mask. His clenched fists are wrapped in studded leather and you notice that his knee-high boots have steel toecaps. When you step out of the car, he starts to snort like an angry bull. As you walk forward to fight the Animal, Amber shouts her encouragement to you.

THE ANIMAL   SKILL 11   STAMINA 16

Resolve this fight to the death using the Hand Fighting rules. The Animal's studded fists reduce STAMINA by 2 points. If you possess knuckle-dusters, you will also reduce STAMINA by 2 points. Otherwise only 1 point will be deducted from the Animal's STAMINA if you win an Attack Round. If you win the fight, turn to 355.

270

You reverse your car to give yourself a long enough run-up to the bridge. You tense slightly, and the adrenalin starts to flow through your veins. The engine roars as you pump the accelerator; then you suddenly release the clutch and screech away to-

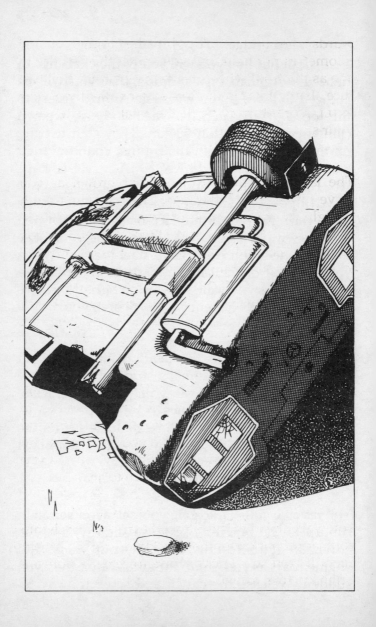

wards the bridge. You hit the bridge at 120 kilometres per hour and you watch the dial rise to 130 as the front wheels leave the ground. Roll two dice. If the total is the same as or less than your SKILL score, turn to **70**. If the total is greater than your SKILL score, turn to **231**.

271

The landscape turns to a reddish-brown as you drive further into the desert. The road runs south straight as an arrow and is virtually clear of abandoned cars. As you drive along, something you recognize catches your eye. It is an overturned Interceptor which must have veered off the road and rolled over after its driver died at the wheel. If you wish to stop to see if there are any spares worth taking, turn to **166**. If you would rather keep on driving, turn to **13**.

272

The road cuts through overgrown fields, but there are no obstructions. You check your milometer to see how far you have come and notice that the petrol gauge is reading empty again. If you have picked up a full fuel canister during your journey, turn to **323**. If you have not picked one up, turn to **364**.

273

You walk ahead of the tattooed man and reach into your jacket pocket for the knuckle-dusters. *Test your Luck*. If you are Lucky, turn to **170**. If you are Unlucky, turn to **250**.

274

A man suddenly appears out of a doorway and walks towards you with his shotgun pointed at you. He looks at you sternly and says, 'That's where I'm heading. Been cycling for over a week since my station-wagon was ambushed and my wife and son were killed. Stopped here to get some cans of food from a supermarket back there, when some crazy dogs attacked me. Shot one of them and the others ran off. My name's Johnson. Pleased to meet you.' He puts down his shotgun and extends his hand for you to shake. He tells you that he is a builder by trade and asks how much further it is to New Hope, and whether he is likely to be let in. You reply that it is only another fifteen kilometres and his chances are good – they need skilled people. You also tell him about your mission and he warns you not to stop at Joe's Garage which is about eight kilometres out of town. 'They ain't got no petrol. They just rob people who stop there.' You thank Johnson for the advice, wish him luck and walk back to your Interceptor. Its powerful engine roars into life when you turn the ignition key, and you screech off once again (turn to 34).

275

You start to feel dizzy and to shiver uncontrollably. You are forced to stop, not feeling capable of driving any further. With horror, you discover swellings on your body caused by the bites of rat fleas infected with plague! You know that the plague is acutely infectious and realize what must be done. You abandon the tanker and set off across country to die, a lone hero. You leave a note written in shaky handwriting on the seat, telling the citizens of your ill fate. A statue in your honour will be erected in the year to come, but you will never see it.

276

You pull off the road and park the Interceptor behind a row of bushes. When you turn the engine off, you suddenly realize how quiet it is outside and wonder if anybody heard you stop. You decide not to go to sleep until it is totally dark, and spend a long time eating your makeshift evening meal. When you are finally convinced that nobody is now likely to find you, you stretch out and go to sleep. In the morning you wake early, feeling refreshed. Add 2 STAMINA points. You waste no time and drive back on the the road to head south (turn to 128).

277

The boot flies open and inside you find a bullet-proof vest. Add 1 LUCK point and 1 SKILL point. You put it on under your jacket and return to your car to drive on (turn to 49).

278

Driving back to the junction, you become aware of a resonating bumping sound coming from the rear of the car. Steering becomes difficult and you are forced to stop. You climb out and immediately discover the problem – a flat tyre. Lose 1 LUCK point. Reaching into the back of the car, you take hold of

the can of Flat-U-Fix and repair the tyre. You are soon driving west again and arrive at the junction, where you turn left (turn to 311).

279
You are hit in the side by a stray bullet as you run across the open space. Roll 1 die and deduct the number from your STAMINA. If you are still alive, turn to 40.

280
Much to your surprise and annoyance, the driver of the armoured car somehow manages to control the skid and drive through the oil slick. You decide immediately to risk a handbrake turn and meet your enemy head on (turn to 77).

281
With revolver in hand, you jump out of the Interceptor and climb warily up the railway embankment. When you reach the top you look towards the bridge and see your attacker grab a bag from out of a caravan abandoned there. He jumps on a motor bike and roars off east away from you. If you wish to look inside the caravan, turn to 58. If you would rather return quickly to the Interceptor to continue the journey, turn to 150.

282

The motor bike swerves from side to side and is a difficult target to hit.

MOTOR BIKE
   and SIDECAR   FIREPOWER 9   ARMOUR 8

If you win this highway battle, turn to **143**.

283

One of the bikers walks over and picks up your revolver and keys. He then tells you to stand up and turn around. He raises his hand and brings the butt of the revolver down hard on the back of your head, knocking you unconscious (turn to **100**).

284

The three cars gradually close up on you, and the one in the lead, a Toyota, begins firing the machine-guns mounted in its headlight compartments.

	FIREPOWER	ARMOUR
TOYOTA	9	15
E-TYPE JAGUAR	10	12
COMMODORE	8	13

Fight each car one at a time. If you win this Vehicle Combat, turn to **265**.

285

You dive at the robed man and pull him to the ground. Rolling over, you put out the lighted match and prevent the incineration of your car. Add 1 LUCK point. Cursing you at the top of his voice, the

man runs off. You let him go: the protection of the Interceptor against other possible maniacs is more important. You waste no more time and drive off south (turn to **254**).

286

When you turn to walk towards the motel again, you notice a dim light shining in one of the upstairs windows: your gunfire has disturbed somebody. You decide not to risk any further confrontation and walk quickly back to the petrol tanker. You drive a few miles further up the road before finding somewhere else suitable to park, and stay inside the cabin to sleep (turn to **218**).

287

The Ford driver is watching you carefully, and turns his car towards the Interceptor as you try to overtake. His front ram bars smash into the side of the Interceptor, punching a hole in the door. Lose 2 ARMOUR points. You keep your foot pressed down on the accelerator and just manage to squeeze in front of the Ford (turn to **340**).

288

The man looks at you long and hard before saying, 'OK, I believe you, but tell me some more.' You explain that you are not the person who killed his wife and son, and had only lied about being a road warrior to keep the whereabouts of New Hope a secret in case the man might lead a raid on it. The man looks suddenly excited and says, 'New Hope, you say? That's where I'm headed. Been cycling in that direction ever since the ambush. Only stopped here to get some cans of food from a supermarket back there, when some crazy dogs attacked me. Shot one of them and the others ran off. My name's Johnson, and I'm sorry about threatening you like I did, but you can't trust anybody these days.' You smile and shake hands, and he tells you that he is a builder by trade. He asks how much further it is to New Hope, and whether he is likely to be let in. You reply that it is only another fifteen kilometres and his chances are good – they need skilled people. You also tell him about your mission and he warns you not to stop at Joe's Garage which is about eight kilometres out of town. 'They ain't got no petrol. They just rob people who stop there.' You thank Johnson for the advice, wish him luck and walk back to the Interceptor. Its powerful engine roars into life when you turn the ignition key, and you screech off once again (turn to 34).

289

You fire rapidly at the advancing vehicle, but cannot see anything except for the blinding lights. Your bullets fail to hit their target, unlike the Animal's machine-gunner. You are an easy target and have no defence against the deadly salvo. You have failed in your mission.

290

The wheels spin in a cloud of smoke as the rubber grips the surface of the road. You control the skid perfectly and are now accelerating towards the oncoming armoured car, which starts to spit bullets at you from its machine-gun.

ARMOURED CAR　　FIREPOWER 9　　ARMOUR 20

If you win, turn to **106**.

291

The masked man reaches into the cabin of the bus and brings out a mahogany box. Inside are two magnificent pistols. He places one bullet in each hand and says, 'Choose your weapon.' You pick up one pistol and balance it in your hand to get a feel for its weight. You both then stand back to back and the man tells you to walk ten paces, turn, and fire when ready. You breathe in deeply and count out loud the ten paces walked. You then turn and see the masked man with his pistol pointed straight at you. Both of you fire at once.

DUELLIST   SKILL 9   STAMINA 9

Carry out one Attack Round using the Shooting rules. If you survive the duel, turn to **208**.

292

If you have a rocket left to fire, turn to **31**. If you do not have a rocket left in your armoury, turn to **173**.

293

If you possess a pair of knuckle-dusters, turn to **56**. If you do not possess a pair of knuckle-dusters, turn to **125**.

294

Still racing, you see ahead of you the white house where you must turn round. You jam on the brakes and turn the steering-wheel sharply to the left. You reverse for a few metres in a cloud of churned-up dust, and then slam the gearstick forwards into first

to race back to the finishing-line. The Ford makes an equally swift U-turn and is soon right behind you again. It powers alongside you, and the driver pulls down on his steering-wheel in order to sideswipe the Interceptor. He looks set to determine the outcome of this duel by ramming.

YELLOW FORD   FIREPOWER 8   ARMOUR 16

A successful ram will reduce a car's ARMOUR by 2 points. If you survive four Attack Rounds, turn to **334**.

295

The car slides to a halt in a cloud of dust. In your rearview-mirror you watch the two bikers run for cover with the mine about to explode. Then it blows, wrecking a wheel, but sounds no louder than a dull thud to you sitting inside the car. Lose 2 ARMOUR points. No sooner has the dust settled than the bikers start to open fire with their motor-cycle machine-guns. You are a sitting target. Roll 1 die and deduct the number from your ARMOUR score. You decide you will have to leave the car to deal with them. You pull the Interceptor's own machine-gun trigger and dive out under the cover of the burst of fire. You scramble behind a nearby bush, revolver drawn, wondering if you were seen. *Test your Luck*.

If you are Lucky, turn to **122**. If you are Unlucky, turn to **329**.

296
The man takes hold of his gun and shoots you at point-blank range. If you are wearing a bullet-proof vest, turn to **174**. If you are not wearing one, turn to **263**.

297
You wake the next morning with a sore arm, but feel somewhat better. Add 2 STAMINA points. If you wish to search the café, turn to **26**. If you would rather drive off immediately, turn to **254**.

298
You drive along the edge of the desert for about eighty kilometres, until the road ends at a T-junction. You decide to turn left and head south into the desert towards San Anglo (turn to **271**).

299
Despite the force of the blast, you only suffer a minor flesh wound caused by flying shrapnel. Lose 2 STAMINA points. You roll along the ground, taking cover behind the Interceptor as your assailants begin shooting. The only way to escape is to shoot it out.

	SKILL	STAMINA
First BIKER	7	13
Second BIKER	5	14

During this Shooting Combat, both bikers will fire separately at you during each Attack Round, but you must choose which of the two you will fire at. Against the other you will throw for your Attack Strength in the normal way, but you will not wound him if your Attack Strength is greater – you must just count this as though his bullet missed you. If you win, turn to **97**, but reduce your SKILL permanently by 1 point if you are shot more than once in the battle.

300

Following the instructions of the tattooed man, you drive down the dirt road to the burnt-out house. Four customized cars are parked in a row, each sprouting a multitude of weapons. A group of people stands in heated discussion, although they all turn to watch you park. You walk over to the group and ask them about the forthcoming race. A small man, with a scar running the length of his face, smiles and says, 'Rookie, huh? Never been to a Blitz Race before? Listen, it's quite simple. Challenge any of us to a race. You have to bet 200 Creds, but if you win, the prize is a big can of petrol! If you win, that is.' The man then bursts into laughter and the others join in. If you wish to challenge him to a Blitz Race, turn to **240**. If you would rather just spectate, turn to **224**.

301

After thirty kilometres or so, the road suddenly ends. Road-construction vehicles stand idle, left to the ravages of the desert heat and wind; there is no sign of life. The road you are driving along was never finished before the catastrophe. Lose 1 LUCK point. To your left, the terrain is flat and stony. To your right and straight ahead there is nothing but sand. If you wish to head east across the stony ground, turn to **251**. If you would rather continue south across the sand, turn to **237**.

302

You open the door and climb out of the Interceptor. As you walk up to the girl, a man with a shaved head jumps out from behind one of the pumps holding a crowbar and shouts, 'Surprise! Let's have your keys and Creds. No funny business unless you want to get hurt.' If you wish to give him your car keys and Credits, turn to **209**. If you would rather fight him with your knife, turn to **48**.

303

As the morning wears on, it becomes very hot and, the further south you travel, you notice a change in the vegetation. The overgrown fields turn into scrubland, and it won't be long before you are driving across the desert. A few miles further down the road, you arrive at a major junction. If you wish to turn left to head east, turn to **140**. If you would rather keep driving south, turn to **189**.

304

As you slow down, a man suddenly appears from out of the ditch by the side of the road. He looks set to throw a bottle at the Interceptor and you can see from the flame-lit rag that it is a petrol bomb. Fortunately only one tyre is punctured and you are able to accelerate and escape the bomber. Further down the road, however, steering becomes difficult and you are forced to stop to inspect the flat tyre. *Test your Luck.* If you are Lucky, turn to **238**. If you are Unlucky, turn to **370**.

305

The helicopter plunges to the ground and bursts into flame on impact. There is nothing you can do but start up your engine and continue west (turn to **216**).

306

You place an empty petrol canister under the truck's petrol tank and connect them with the plastic tubing. You suck the tube to start the petrol flowing. You siphon out all of the tank's petrol, nearly filling your canister. Add 1 LUCK point. You place the fuel inside the Interceptor and continue the drive south (turn to **118**).

307

You walk over to the bikers' motor cycle and notice a locked side-pannier. If you wish to open the pannier, turn to **206**. If you would rather change the wheel on your Interceptor, without wasting any more time, turn to **346**.

308

Your shot is accurate and the wolf is dead before it hits the ground. The remaining wolf is scared off by the shot and disappears into the shadows (turn to **286**).

309

You watch the bike speed away into the distance until it disappears from view. After waiting for a few minutes you set off east once again. You soon come to a signpost which points down a narrow dirt track towards a town called Rockville. If you wish to drive south to Rockville, turn to **157**. If you would rather keep heading east, turn to **45**.

310

You stop the car and pour the contents of the can into the petrol tank. You know that you do not have

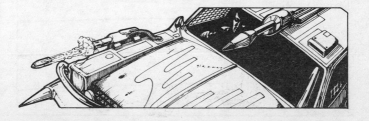

enough fuel to reach San Anglo and wonder where you will find some more in this desert wilderness. It is a depressing thought which weighs on your mind as you set off again (turn to 115).

311

A few miles down the road you come to a small, crudely constructed wooden bridge which crosses a narrow river. There is a sign nailed to the bridge warning you not to cross the river. If you intend to drive across regardless, turn to 229. If you would rather turn around and drive back to the last junction, turn to 124.

312

You press the button on the dashboard which releases the canister. The iron spikes are spread all over the road and you watch the armoured car drive towards them in your mirror. *Test your Luck.* If you are Lucky, turn to 181. If you are Unlucky, turn to 41.

313

You are able to inflate one of the tyres with the can of Flat-U-Fix, but the other is damaged beyond repair. If you possess a spare wheel, turn to 19. If you have already used both spare wheels, turn to 336.

314

You screech to a halt and push the gearstick into reverse. The rocks and boulders crash down on to the road in front of you, but none lands on top of the car. Add 1 LUCK point. Fortunately the landslide is not heavy enough to block the road completely, and you are soon able to drive on (turn to 351).

315
Somebody has fired a bazooka at you and it is a direct hit. Roll two dice and deduct the total from the Interceptor's ARMOUR. If you survive the blast, turn to 53.

316
In silence, the Doom Dogs carry the Animal over to the station-wagon and place him in the back. By the time the two vehicles are unlocked from each other, the sun is rising above the eastern horizon. You are bathed in warm red light and feel suddenly optimistic about completing the mission. You drive off south, leaving the Doom Dogs behind (turn to 90).

317
You drive off the road on to the rocky scrubland and are suddenly surprised by the sight of two vicious-looking leather-clad bikers who jump out from behind a bush. One fires a shot from his pistol to give cover to the other who slams a limpet mine against the rear wheel-arch of your Interceptor. Lose 1 LUCK point. They dive for cover before you even think about firing your machine-gun. Your mind races in panic as you decide what to do. Will you:

Keep on driving?	Turn to **17**
Stop the car and jump out?	Turn to **212**
Stop the car and stay inside?	Turn to **295**

318

You press the button on the dashboard which releases the canister. You watch it bounce along the road as the Ford speeds towards it. *Test your Luck.* If you are Lucky, turn to **63**. If you are Unlucky, turn to **98**.

319

Amber hands you some glucose tablets and energy synthi-pills. Add 4 STAMINA points. Turn to **32**.

320

The shell explodes harmlessly some twenty metres behind you, but you know it will not be long before they fire again. What is more, a bullet has punctured one of your front tyres, which forces you to stop. If you have a rocket left to fire, turn to **31**. If you do not have a rocket left in your armoury, turn to **173**.

321

The first building you come to is an old roadside café. There are cars on the forecourt, but none looks as though they have been driven since the catastrophe. You drive around the back to hide the Interceptor. After climbing out and looking around to make sure that nobody else is staying here, you decide where to sleep. If you wish to sleep in the bed in the room above the café, turn to **55**. If you wish to sleep in the wooden outhouse, turn to **332**.

322

The E-type Jaguar races across the finishing-line ahead of you and is greeted by six cheering people. Leonardi swerves the E-type across the road to stop you driving past, and signals for you to stop. If you wish to obey him, turn to **378**. If you would rather risk swerving around the E-type and trying to make a getaway, turn to **162**.

323

You brake to a halt and get out of the car to empty the fuel canister into the petrol tank. The canister does not hold much petrol and you realize that you will have to be on the look-out for more if you hope to reach San Anglo. By the time you set off again, it is early evening and you watch the setting sun through the right-hand window. Soon it will be dark and there is a new decision to make. If you wish to drive off the road to sleep the night inside the Interceptor, turn to **276**. If you would rather drive through the night, turn to **42**.

324

Your rapid-firing machine-gun does not miss its target and the bike runs off the road, crashing into a tree. But the rider does not die in vain – his crossbow bolt pierces your front tyre, sending the tanker into an uncontrollable spin. You wrestle with the steering-wheel, but cannot stop the tanker from jack-knifing. The trailer swings round and suddenly the whole tanker flips over on its side, screeching to a sudden halt in a shower of sparks. Trapped inside the cabin, you realize that you have failed in your mission, and you will be lucky even to escape with your life, as the other motor bike is drawing alongside . . .

325

You throw your revolver into the sand beyond the ambulance. A pair of leather boots comes into sight, and you see a hand reach down and pick up the revolver. You crawl out and stand up with your arms raised. A scruffy man stands in front of you, pointing his gun straight at you. A cigar hangs out of the corner of his moustached mouth and he stares at you coldly, the sun kept out of his eyes by a red headband. He orders you to throw over the keys to your Interceptor. If you wish to obey him, turn to **366**. If you wish to reach for your knife to throw it at him, turn to **82**.

326

You run as fast as you can, glancing several times over your shoulder to watch the vehicle circling the hill, trying to pick up your tracks. You are still some distance away from the Interceptor when your trail is found and the vehicle turns to give chase. An angry voice booms out over the desert through a loudspeaker, shouting, 'Stop! There is no escape from the Animal.' The message is repeated over and over again, growing louder as the vehicle catches up with you. There is no hope of reaching the Interceptor and you yell at Amber to lie down and shoot at the vehicle, aiming at its headlights. Roll two dice. If the total is the same as or less than your SKILL, turn to **113**. If the total is greater than your SKILL, turn to **289**.

327

You decide to wait until morning before driving any further. You wake early, but the short rest has done you some good. Add 1 STAMINA point. After reversing the Interceptor out of the wreckage, you once again drive off south down the road (turn to **254**).

328

You release the canister and watch with satisfaction as two of the cars collide. The remaining one, a Toyota, continues the chase and opens fire with the machine-guns mounted in its headlight compartments.

TOYOTA   FIREPOWER 9   ARMOUR 15

If you win this Vehicle Combat, turn to **265**.

329

One of the bikers saw you when you jumped for cover. He calls out to you, saying, 'Throw out your gun and keys. We only want your car.' If you wish to obey him, turn to **283**. If you would rather fight it out, turn to **6**.

330

You turn the Interceptor around and drive back to the wooden gate where the guard stands, pointing his machine-gun at you. 'Changed your mind, huh?' he sneers. You nod slowly, not wishing to show your anger. He opens the gate, reminding you where to go (turn to **300**).

331

Amber suddenly lets out a warning cry and points at a Jeep driving fast down the road towards you. 'Doom Dogs!' she cries. 'The same ones that attacked me before.' The Jeep has a twin-barrelled machine-gun mounted in a turret at the back, and its operator begins firing as soon as you are in range.

JEEP   FIREPOWER 9   ARMOUR 14

If you win this Vehicle Combat, turn to **7**.

332

The outhouse is dark and warm. You make yourself a place to sleep between logs that were collected for the café's fireplace. As the light fades, you eat some of your rations and ponder the events of the day. Perhaps tomorrow you will reach San Anglo. When it is completely dark you settle down to sleep. *Test your Luck*. If you are Lucky, turn to **16**. If you are Unlucky, turn to **84**.

333

Roll two dice. If the total is the same as or less than your SKILL score, turn to **57**. If the total is greater than your SKILL score, turn to **86**.

334

There is probably about a kilometre to go before you cross the finishing-line, and you are still locked in combat alongside the Ford. Up ahead the road narrows to one lane to cross a stone bridge spanning a stream. If you wish to keep your accelerator pressed to the floor, turn to **35**. If you would rather ease off the accelerator and allow the Ford to take the lead, turn to **239**.

335

It is a dark night and you need to use your torch to see where you are going. *Test your Luck*. If you are Lucky, turn to **5**. If you are Unlucky, turn to **365**.

336

It is impossible to drive on the shredded tyre any longer. You look around forlornly at the deserted countryside and realize that nobody will come to your aid. You will have to try your best to get back to New Hope on foot. You have failed in your mission.

337
You are soon back at the junction at the foot of the hills, but carry straight on to head west (turn to **211**).

338
As you close in on the farmhouse you see another blinding flash; the bazooka is being fired from a top-floor window. You swerve violently to the left to avoid the exploding shell. *Test your Luck.* If you are Lucky, turn to **320**. If you are Unlucky, turn to **105**.

339
You crawl to the gate unnoticed, and slip inside the vehicle compound. Amber moves from vehicle to vehicle, attaching small limpet mines to their engine-blocks. When she has finished activating them, she signals for you to leave. You crawl down the side of the hill and stand up to run when you feel you are out of sight. The explosions suddenly start, and you count seven in all. 'One of the mines must have had a faulty fuse,' Amber says breathlessly as you run back towards the Interceptor. You hear an engine start and look behind you to see two beams of light moving away from the rising flames of the burning wrecks. The Doom Dogs intend to hunt down their attackers. If your current STAMINA is 10 or greater, turn to **107**. If your current STAMINA is less than 10, turn to **326**.

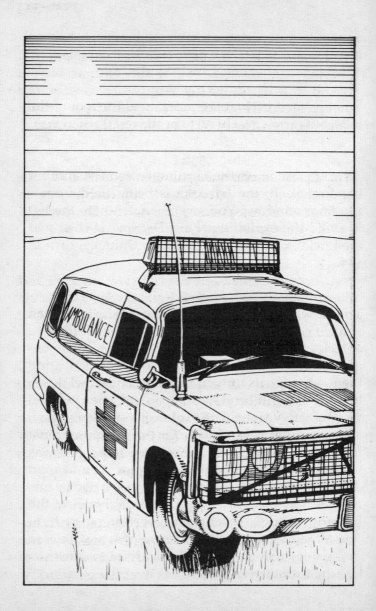

340

You decide that it is time to use a weapon against the chasing car, so you look at the buttons on the dashboard. If you wish to empty a canister of iron spikes on to the road, turn to **318**. If you would rather spray a film of oil over the road, turn to **213**.

341

You pass an ambulance parked off the road to your right, but see no sign of life. If you wish to stop to investigate the ambulance, turn to **267**. If you would rather keep driving east, turn to **22**.

342

You do not manage to swerve away in time and crash into the stone pillar. Roll one die and deduct the number from your car's ARMOUR. If you survive the crash, turn to **79**.

343

You curse your luck, but there is nothing you can do about the ruined tyre. It is impossible to drive on it any further over the desert terrain and you realize that you will have to abandon the Interceptor. With luck you will make it back to New Hope, and try to reach San Anglo again another time.

344

You drive back down the road, passing the ambulance on your left and crossing the highway you came off some time ago. The road is relatively free of obstacles and you are able to travel along it quickly.

However, the easy drive is shortlived. The road comes to a river, which it used to cross, but the drawbridge, which spans the river, is partly open, stopping you from driving across it. You reckon that if you drive over it at about 130 kilometres per hour, the momentum should carry the Interceptor across the gap to the far side. You decide to give it a try (turn to 270).

345

The crossbow bolt flies past your head, much to the annoyance of the hijacker. You jump on top of the trailer, and run forward to wrestle with the man before he has time to reload his crossbow. Roll 1 die and add the number to your current SKILL score. Roll the die again and add the number to the hijacker's SKILL of 7. If your total is the same as or greater than that of the hijacker, turn to 74. If your total is lower than that of the hijacker, turn to 226.

346

Fortunately the wheel-hub is not damaged and you are able to fit the spare wheel quite quickly. You are soon charging down the road, shaking your head at the mad world you are forced to live in. You soon arrive at another signpost which points down a narrow dirt track towards a town called Rockville. If you wish to drive south to Rockville, turn to 157. If you would rather keep heading east, turn to 45.

347

The tattooed man is slow to realize your trick, and takes the full force of your improvised karate kick in the stomach. He crumples to the floor, giving you time to run to the Interceptor. As you open the door, the man recovers enough to fire a burst from his machine-gun at you. *Test your Luck*. If you are Lucky, turn to **204**. If you are Unlucky, turn to **65**.

348

You decide against driving any further during the night, and settle down for a short nap before dawn breaks. You instinctively wake as the first rays of sunshine creep over the horizon. Add 1 STAMINA point. You survey the damage to the Interceptor and find that, apart from a slight steering problem, it is sound enough to drive. You jump back inside and set off south, thankful that there are no vehicle road-worthiness inspectors around any more (turn to **128**).

349

You manage to knock the guard unconscious and catch him as he falls, hoping that his friends do not notice what is happening. You tie him up with his own belt and leave him on the hillside. It won't be long before he is missed, so you scramble quickly up the hill to the fence (turn to **198**).

350

The shot misses and the dog closes in and leaps at you. Quickly you draw your knife to defend yourself.

WILD DOG   SKILL 7   STAMINA 5

Use the Hand Fighting rules to resolve this combat

(to the death). Your knife and the dog's bite both reduce STAMINA by 2 points. If you win, turn to **89**.

351

The road eventually leads out of the canyon, continuing straight on as far as the eye can see. You check your compass and see that you are travelling south once again. However, you have only driven for a few kilometres, when you are forced to stop by a blockade of two cars parked across the road. Two armed men in leather uniforms approach you on foot and tell you that the only way you will be allowed to drive any further south is to win a speed race along the straight road, against their ace driver. If you lose the race, you will be forced to turn back. Suddenly a car draws up alongside the Interceptor. You recognize the classic car of last century immediately: it is an E-type Jaguar. Sitting in the driver's seat is a thin man with short black hair. He looks very self-assured, and says, 'Hi, my name's Leonardi. I used to play ball for the Mets, but now I race cars. Too bad you are driving that old trash can, but good luck anyway.' The two cars blocking the road are moved aside and you see several more cars beyond them lining the road. A man appears with a flag ready to start the race. He lowers it sharply and the race begins while you are still trying to grasp what is happening. The E-type screeches away slightly ahead of you. If you have had a supercharger fitted to your engine, turn to **210**. If you have not had one fitted, turn to **358**.

352

The wheels spin in a cloud of smoke as the rubber tries to grip the surface of the road. But you have overdone it, and the car spins into a shallow ditch by the side of the road. The armoured car closes in and suddenly you see the flash of machine-gun fire spitting from its turret.

ARMOURED CAR   FIREPOWER 9   ARMOUR 20

During this Vehicle Combat reduce your FIRE-POWER by 2 because of your car's immobility. If you win, turn to 33.

353

The dirt track twists and turns through the open countryside, but at last you come to a T-junction where the dirt track is crossed by a good road. You look down it both ways, but do not see any vehicles or signs of life. If you wish to head east, turn to 61. If you wish to head west, turn to 371.

354

The Interceptor swerves to the left, but you steer into the skid and keep the car under control. You have to think quickly to decide what tactics to use. Will you accelerate away (turn to 183), or brake hard to let the Ford pass you (turn to 27)?

355

The Doom Dogs suddenly stop their cheering when the Animal fails to get up from the sand. They look at one another, obviously deciding whether or not to let you go, despite their promise. *Test your Luck*. If you are Lucky, turn to **316**. If you are Unlucky, turn to **184**.

356

Lying perfectly still under the ambulance, you hear the sound of footsteps approaching. The pain in your side is severe, making you grip your revolver tightly. Suddenly a man's voice shouts, 'Hey, stupid, think I can't follow a trail of blood? Throw your gun out and ease yourself out from under that ambulance with your hands up.' If you wish to obey him, turn to **325**. If you wish to roll out from under the ambulance firing your gun, turn to **12**.

357

Stranded in a desert wilderness, hundreds of kilometres from medical aid, there is nothing you can do to stop the deadly poison spreading through your body. You soon begin to feel very weak, unable even to summon enough strength to drive. It is not long before the poison runs its fatal course. Your adventure ends here.

358

Roll one die alternately, for the E-type and then for the Interceptor. Continue rolling until one car reaches a total of 24 to cross the finishing-line first. If you win, turn to **54**. If you lose the race, turn to **322**.

359

Inside the boot of an old Ford you find something which makes you whoop for joy – a full canister of petrol. Add 1 LUCK point. Carrying the crowbar and fuel canister, you leap across the roofs of the cars to hurry back to the Interceptor. Luckily it is still where you left it and you are soon on the road again, heading south (turn to **149**).

360

Amber swings and misses again, but you are able to free your arms while you roll over in the sand. The Animal continues to squeeze as you try to grab him around the throat. Lose 2 STAMINA points. With his head held in position, Amber does not miss with the spanner this time (turn to **376**).

361

You press the release button which empties the canister of oil in a thick spray over the road. The motor-cycle combination runs over the oil at high speed and skids off the road. It rolls over in the sand and disappears from view, as you drive away (turn to **96**).

362

The country road runs straight ahead far into the distance and you are able to make good headway, as it is relatively free from abandoned cars. But after an hour's driving at high speed, the road finally ends at a T-junction. If you wish to turn left, turn to **92**. If you wish to turn right, turn to **153**.

363

The man reacts too slowly to dodge the blow and crumples to the floor unconscious. You run as fast as you can to the Interceptor to escape before his friends realize what has happened. Much to your relief, the Interceptor starts first time, and you screech away down the rough road to the main road where you turn right at speed to head south (turn to **207**).

364

A few kilometres further down the road, the engine starts to cough and splutter. Finally it jerks to a halt and your worst fears are realized – you have run out of petrol. There are no buildings and no signs of life, and you realize that the mission is over. You have failed, and must try to get back to New Hope on foot, perhaps to try to reach San Anglo another time.

365

As you walk across the courtyard towards the motel, you suddenly hear a howling cry behind you. You spin round and see two pairs of eyes caught in the beam of your torch. You see that they belong to two wolves, who leap forward to attack. You quickly draw your gun and aim at the leading wolf. Roll two dice. If the total is the same as or less than your SKILL, turn to **308**. If the total is greater than your SKILL, turn to **120**.

366

The man orders you to turn around and then hits you over the back of the head with the butt of his gun. You drop unconscious to the floor, and when you awake you find that the man – and your Interceptor – are gone. You have failed in your mission.

367

The man suddenly sees you and calls to his friends, 'Hey, everybody, guess what? We've got visitors.' Pointing his rifle at you, he orders you to stand up

and put your hands in the air. Within seconds you are surrounded by ten Doom Dogs. Your fate rests with this gang of desert outlaws; your mission will never be completed.

368

As you pull the dagger from your side, your attacker draws a small revolver from his concealed shoulder-holster. You will have to fight this out.

BANDIT   SKILL 7   STAMINA 11

Resolve this combat using the Shooting rules, but add 1 point to your own SKILL for the duration of the battle because of your cover behind the car door. If you win, turn to **64**, but reduce your SKILL permanently by 1 point if you are shot more than once.

369

The masked man takes the 200 Credits from you and then reverses the bus to let you enter the tunnel. You soon pass through it and find yourself driving along a twisting road which cuts through the bottom of a deep canyon (turn to **130**).

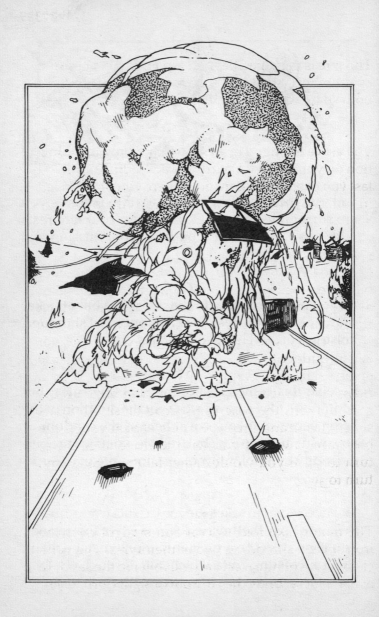

370

The tyre is damaged beyond repair. If you possess a spare wheel, turn to **19**. If you have already used both spare wheels, turn to **336**.

371

You drive a long way west, passing only one junction on your right – a narrow road leading north. At last you come to a T-junction where you can turn left in order to drive south towards San Anglo (turn to **225**).

372

Reaching forward, you press the rocket-launcher button on the control panel. The Interceptor shakes as the rocket is fired, and the explosion which follows immediately is loud and blinding. When the smoke clears, you see that the road-block no longer exists. Suddenly you hear the roar of a motor-cycle engine starting up and see two leather-clad, armed riders appear from behind a bush and blaze up the road through the hole in the road-block. The passenger turns and fires a warning shot at you as the bike races away. If you wish to drive after them, turn to **95**. If you would rather let them get away, turn to **309**.

373

The motor bike and sidecar run straight over the iron spikes, shredding two of their tyres. The vehicle swerves off the road and rolls over in the sand. In a matter of seconds they are out of sight (turn to **96**).

374

You draw your knife and ready yourself as the dog leaps at you.

WILD DOG   SKILL 7   STAMINA 5

Use the Hand Fighting rules to resolve this combat (to the death). Your knife and the dog's bite both reduce STAMINA by 2 points. If you win, turn to **89**.

375

You decide to take the outlaw's Magnum as it is a deadlier weapon than your own revolver. Add 1 SKILL point for all future Shooting Combats. You turn the ignition key and the engine roars into life. Soon you are travelling south again at high speed (turn to **303**).

376

The Animal is knocked unconscious, but you take no chances and tie his hands. By the time you manage to free the Interceptor from the station-wagon, the sun is rising above the eastern horizon. You are bathed in warm red light and feel suddenly optimistic about completing the mission. You drive off south, leaving the cursing Animal to be found by the rest of his gang (turn to **90**).

377

You swerve the car from side to side to make it difficult to aim at, and at the same time return fire with your machine-gun. Roll two dice. If the total is the same as or less than your SKILL, turn to 338. If the total is greater than your SKILL, turn to 191.

378

Leonardi climbs out of the E-type, walks over to the Interceptor and says, 'You're good, but you're just not good enough. You'd better turn around now and head back towards the canyon.' You do as he says and are soon back on the twisting road through the canyon. You pass the landslide and enter the tunnel. Much to your surprise you see daylight at the end and drive through it unhindered. A mile further on down the road you see the bus that was blocking the tunnel before. You overtake it without incident and drive on until you reach the T-junction. You turn left to head south along the straight desert road (turn to 301).

379

When you are only a few metres from the bridge, the Ford driver's courage deserts him and he brakes hard, allowing you to cross ahead of him. Frustrated by your iron nerve, your opponent desperately tries to pass you before you cross the finishing-line. The acceleration of the Ford is blistering because of its supercharger, and the cars are soon locked bumper to bumper. You see the finishing-line ahead, no more than two hundred metres away, and realize that the Ford will pull out of your slipstream any second now to pass you. You must block the Ford. Will you swerve to the left (turn to **20**) or to the right (turn to **80**)?

380

You drive on towards New Hope, and are relieved to see the town gates open. Hundreds of citizens turn out to greet you, and you are given a hero's reception. The petrol will be put to good use to help build for the future. Civilization, albeit in a small way, is on the road to recovery. If you also managed to rescue Sinclair during your adventure, consider your mission a triumph.

THE TROLLTOOTH WARS

Steve Jackson

It started with an ambush. When Balthus Dire's blood-lusting Hill Goblins mount their raid on the Strongarm caravan, little do they realize what dramatic consequences their actions will have. For that caravan carries Cunnelwort, a mystical herb from Eastern Allansia, destined for none other than the evil sorceror, Zharradan Marr! War – between two forces well-matched for evil – is soon to ensue ... Will Balthus Dire's chaotics or Zharradan Marr's undead prove victorious? The answer is here, in the first Fighting Fantasy novel.

DEMONSTEALER

Marc Gascoigne

It started with a burglary. Borne aloft on the back of an immense bat, a sinister thief breaks into the tower of the sorcerer Yaztromo. Guided by long-dead voices, he manages to make off with an ancient scroll whose secrets could spell doom and destruction for all Allansia!

Chadda Darkmane is soon on the trail of the thief. But as the quest grows ever longer, his nagging doubts about the power of sorcery turn into nightmares. The trail leads far beyond northern Allansia, to the Pirate Coast and the twisting alleyways of Rimon, where Darkmane's nightmares become flesh! For the thief has used the ancient scroll to summon others to help him in his sorcerous task, Demons who are not bound by the constraints of earthly forms – who feast on the human spirit.

A few brave companions accompany Darkmane, but will they be enough – and in time – to stop the thief from unlocking the final secret of Yaztromo's scroll? *Demonstealer*, the second Fighting Fantasy novel in a series that began with *The Trolltooth Wars*, holds all the answers.

FIGHTING FANTASY
The Introductory Role-playing Game
Steve Jackson

Thrilling adventures of sword and sorcery come to life in the Fighting Fantasy Gamebooks, where the reader is the hero, dicing with death and demons in search of villains, treasure or freedom. Now YOU can create your own Fighting Fantasy adventures and send your friends off on dangerous missions! In this clearly written handbook there are hints on devising combats, monsters to use, tricks and tactics, as well as two mini-adventures.

THE RIDDLING REAVER
Steve Jackson

Four Fighting Fantasy episodes to be played as separate adventures or as stages in an epic adventure, *The Riddling Reaver* is a rival worthy of the most daring adventurers. His mind is inscrutable — but there is no doubt about the chaos he plans to unleash on the world. He *must* be stopped, despite the hazards of the task!

A follow-up to *Fighting Fantasy: The Introductory Role-playing Game*, it contains instructions and scenarios so that you can conjure up adventures for your friends and send them on their most dangerous and puzzling mission yet.

OUT OF THE PIT
Fighting Fantasy Monsters
Steve Jackson and Ian Livingstone

From the darkest corners, from the deepest pools and from the dungeons thought only to exist in nightmares come the Fighting Fantasy monsters — the downfall of many a brave warrior. Two hundred and fifty of these loathsome creatures from the wild and dangerous worlds of Fighting Fantasy are collected here — some are old adversaries, many you have yet to meet — each of them described in minute detail. An indispensable guide for Fighting Fantasy adventurers!

TITAN
The Fighting Fantasy World
Steve Jackson and Ian Livingstone
edited by Marc Gascoigne

You met the monsters in *Out of the Pit* now meet the rest of the Fighting Fantasy world! No adventurer should be without this essential guide. It contains everything you need to know, covering the turbulent history of the world, from its creation and early civilizations — through the devastating War of the Wizards — to the present-day wilderness and anarchy where the delicate balance between Good and Chaos could at any moment be overturned.